Corah's Magical Excursions in the Night

by Stanley Longman

Acknowledgements

I am grateful to many people who helped and encouraged the development of these excursions. First among them might be = Longman and her family. Applied Images of Gainesville, Georgia undertook the first printing of this book and Barbara Thomas designed its layout. I value the advice and support of William Bray and Bowen Craig of Bilbo Books. Finally, I am indebted to Dan Roth of Athens Creative Design for his layout that brought the book into its present shape.

Table of Contents

Excursion #1:   "Tea Time on an Island" 1

Excursion #2:   "Off to Play Tennis on a Cloud" 11

Excursion #3:   "Off to the Races Under the Sea" 21

Excursion #4:   "In Search of the Unicorn" 31

Excursion #5:   "A Place for Ideas and
                     Stories and Pictures" 45

Excursion #6:   "Flying Up to Mount Parnassus" 55

Excursion #7:   "Castle on the Hilltop" 65

Excursion #8:   "The Mythical Menagerie" 73

Excursion #9:   "Interplanetary Travel" 85

Excursion #10:   "Floating to the Elysian Flields" 97

Excursion #1:

"Tea Time on an Island"

CORAH WAS SOUND ASLEEP IN HER BED. SHE FELL ASLEEP when Daddy was reading her a story about people travel-ing in a boat, but she never heard if the people lived happily ever after. For a little while that bothered her but not enough to stop her falling into a deep slumber. Then something **did** start to bother her. Something strange. It wasn't something shaking her bed. It wasn't a light or a voice. It was just a feeling. Something was happening and it made her open her eyes.

She looked around the room. At first it all seemed just the way it always did. But then she noticed a very strange thing. There was a mist moving along the floor. She sat bolt upright in bed. Where was that mist coming from? Swinging her feet out over the side of the bed, she studied the ground and the gathering mist. Very slowly she stepped down onto the floor. Her feet settled into the mist. It felt cool. Wading through it she came to something really strange: there was a door in her room that was never there before. Now that was really peculiar -- even more so because the mist was seeping in from under the door. She got to studying the door. It was a fine door with a gold handle and panels in its dark wood. Two of the panels seemed to be looking at her, but she couldn't be sure of that.

"You may open me if you like." It seemed like the door said that. But doors don't talk, do they? She never heard a door talk before but who else would say a thing like "You may open me"?

Corah cocked her head. "Did you talk to me just now, door?"

The door laughed making all its panels shake. "Of course I did. Any time someone stands in front of me I like to invite them to come on in."

"Oh," said Corah. "But I don't know what's in there."

"It'll be interesting, I can tell you that."

Corah was a little suspicious. "How do you know?"

"I can see the place. My backside looks all around, you see?" One of the panels winked at Corah.

"Tell me what your backside sees, okay?"

"Just at the moment it's a little hard to say because of all the mist, don't you know?" Another panel winked at Corah.

Now she was really suspicious. "If all you got on the other side is mist, I'm staying right here. There's mist all over my floor. I don't need any more."

"Aw, come on. I like it when people open me. You can do it."

"Nothing doing!" And Corah turned and waded back toward her bed. "I'm going back to sleep. Anyway, you're not real."

"What do you mean, not real? Where do you think all this mist comes from if I'm not real? Huh? Tell me that."

Corah was stumped. Then she said, "Okay, if you're so real, tell me what is out there when there **is** no mist. Your backside must have seen that."

"All right, I'll tell you. What is out there, what is waiting for you, is an excursion."

"An excursion!" Corah exclaimed. "You can't see an excursion. It's not something you see. It's something you do."

"You're right. You're pretty smart. It **is** something you do. Right now it's out there waiting for you to do!"

"For me?"

"Yes. For Corah."

"You know my name? How do you know my name?"

"Of course. I do And you can call me Door. That's my name. Now the excursion is waiting for you. You've been invited for tea."

"Me?"

"Yes. You. Now come open me up."

Corah wasn't sure about this. Very slowly she waded through the mist back to the door. Very slowly she put her hand on the gold handle. Very slowly she pulled it down. And very slowly she cracked the door open, oh so very little, just to get a glimpse of the other side. Suddenly the door threw itself open. Corah was flung through the

air and landed on her bottom. What a shock! She turned and glared at the door. "Door, that wasn't very nice," she complained.

"Sorry but I just can't wait for you to enjoy your excursion. I'll be here when you get back." And Door gently closed itself and clicked shut.

"I don't know if I like this at all," she muttered to herself as she stood up and dusted herself off. She looked around. This certainly was a misty place. You can't see much of anything. She seemed to be on a sort of dock made of wooden planks. That was all. At the far end there was nothing, just more mist. Was it a lake? Maybe an empty space? Or a meadow? How can anyone tell?

"What took you so long?" said a gruff voice. It startled Corah and she couldn't make out where it came from. "I've been waiting for such a long time. And the ladies are expecting you for tea." Now Corah was convinced the voice came from directly over her head. She looked up and sure enough there was a large, round balloon of a man floating in the air over her head.

"Who are you? And why are you floating in the air like that?"

"Oh, do pardon me. I'll come right down. It'll just take mo-ment." With that the man seemed to punch his finger in his belly. There was a hissing sound and gradually he shrank to a normal size and sank slowly to settle on the dock planks next to Corah. "I'm Trilby, Mr. Trilby, your tour director. So glad to meet you." He put out his hand for Corah to shake.

This was much better – Corah preferred talking to a little man on her level than a puffed up man over her head. So she shook his hand and asked, "What does a tour director do?"

"I direct your tours...plan your trips... arrange your expeditions. That's what I do," he proclaimed proudly.

"You mean my excursions."

"That's right, your excursions. Now, what would you like today? You want to fly, float or roll?"

"What do you mean, fly, float or roll?"

"Well, if you choose to fly, we'll put you in a flying machine and have you soar over the land. If you'd rather float, we'll put you in a boat and have you sail on the sea. For rolling, we'll use a vehicle with wheels so you can ride across the landscape. So, what'll it be today?"

Corah liked all those. They seemed very exciting. It'd be nice to do all three. Finally she opted for floating: "Put me in a boat," she announced.

"Right-o!" Trilby got to his feet and walked to the edge of the dock and emitted a shrill whistle. Finally Corah got a good look at Trilby. He wore a bright red jacket with gold braids and a high crowned hat. He had a great walrus mustache and his feet were large webbed flippers. "I'll give you a poem about that. You like poems, don't you, Corah?" Then he stood straight and tall and recited this poem in a singsong voice:

It's a fact worth note
That in order to float
You shall need a boat
And that's just the way it is, don't you know't."

Corah laughed. "That was funny. Your poem just fell apart at the end."

"You're right, " he admitted. "I'll have to work on it some more."

As he said this, a sailboat appeared out of the mist and pulled up at the dock. So, there was water out there. Corah got to wondering, "What if I said I wanted to roll? How could you do that with all that water out there? Tell me that."

"Oh, well," Mr. Trilby shrugged, "then there would be a road out there and a motor car would drive up. Or maybe a railroad track and a choo choo train would pull up at the platform."

"How about if I said I'd fly? What then?"

"Then there would be a runway out there and a plane would land and taxi here to pick you up. Whatever you like, we can take care of it. But you said float and here's your boat. Go ahead. Get in."

Corah got in, but the boat just sat there at the dock. "Isn't the boat going to go somewhere?" she asked.

"Thanks for reminding me. Yes, you're going on an excursion. You're going to meet Mrs. Molmy and Mrs. Balmy. They're holding tea for you on an island far away from here. You'd better hurry."

Corah was getting a little annoyed. "How can I hurry to an island far away when this boat just sits in the water?"

"Oh, I'll take care of that." Mr. Trilby puffed himself back up so he was as big and round as he was when Corah first saw him. Then he opened his mouth and blew a great wind into the boat's sail and suddenly the boat took off at a tremendous speed. Mr. Trilby shouted, "Bon voyage!" and he was out of sight and out of earshot.

As she traveled the mist cleared away and the sun came out. The sky was blue and a light breeze was blowing. The boat kept speeding through the water. The island might have been far away, but Corah got there in a flash. The boat put down its anchor at the base of a high terrace. Corah looked up. Two ladies waved to her from the top of the terrace. One of them surely was Mrs. Molmy and the other Mrs. Balmy, but they looked exactly alike. Who could tell which was which, Corah wondered as she started up the forty-two steps to the terrace. Maybe she would find out, but in fact she never did,

even after sitting with the two of them all through the teatime. They even sounded alike and each repeated what the other spoke. They were very nice, Corah thought, but they sure were strange.

When Corah got to the terrace, the ladies beamed at her and one said, "Welcome, Corah. Nice to meet you," and the other said, "Nice to meet you. Welcome, Corah." Then one lady said, "Come sit down at table. We've got tea and crumpets and cucumber sandwiches and little tea cakes." and the other one said the same things, only backwards: "We've got little tea cakes and cucumber sandwiches and crumpets and tea. Come sit down at table." And the two la-

dies sat down very primly and each spread her napkin carefully on her lap. So Corah sat down in the one chair left and did exactly as they did, spreading her napkin on her lap.

"I'll be mother. I'll pour." And as she did, the other said, "She'll pour. She'll be mother." But then nothing came out of the teapot into Corah's cup. Nothing went into the other cups. And when they offered the cucumber sandwiches, the plate was empty. All the plates were empty. Corah thought it must be some kind of game, so she took an invisible sandwich and put it on her plate and she took a spoonful of sugar and stirred it in her cup. They offered her many

things to eat and she ate them with relish. That was the strangest thing of all -- she was eating nothing and getting full. And it all tasted so good. She stopped and said, "That was very good. Thank you so much." And one replied, "You're most welcome, I'm sure," and the other said, "I'm sure you're most welcome."

By then the sun was setting and Corah thought she should get back to her door. But first she wanted to know, "Which one of you is Mrs. Molmy and which is Mrs. Balmy?" "I'm Mrs. Balmy and she's Mrs. Molmy" and the other said, "I'm Mrs. Molmy and she's Mrs. Balmy," and they pointed at each other. "Or the other way around," "Or vice versa." And then they both said at the same time, "We're really not sure."

"Oh," said Corah as if she understood. "I have to go now. But when I get back in the boat, I don't know how to make it go."

"That's no problem. We'll help." And "We'll help. That's no problem." They walked down the forty-two steps with Corah and at the bottom they took out a large bellows. Corah got in the boat and it raised its anchor. The ladies worked the bellows and it made just the right wind for the boat to take off. Corah heard them say something about "Have a good trip" and "Goodbye," but they were out of sight in a flash.

The boat sped into night. The stars twinkled in the sky and the moon lent its silver beams to the water. Mr. Trilby was there when the boat came to a stop at the dock. "Welcome back," he said as he helped her onto the dock. "Now, wasn't that a wonderful excursion for you? Did you like it?"

"Oh, yes," Corah cried. "But the ladies didn't know which was which and their food was invisible."

"They're always like that." And he took Corah to the door. Door winked one eye and said, "Didn't I tell you'd have an excursion?" Then Door opened itself graciously and Corah went back into her room. She was really tired from her trip and so she climbed into bed and was soon fast asleep.

When she woke in the morning, she remembered that unusual excursion. She sat up in bed and looked to see if the door was still there. It was gone. Then she noticed she was hungry. Perhaps she never really ate any of that invisible food. She ran downstairs to the kitchen. She wanted to ask her mother if she ever saw a door in her room with dark wood paneling, but she decided not to.

Excursion #2:

"Off to Play Tennis on a Cloud"

NOTHING LIKE THE TRIP TO THE ISLAND FOR TEA with Mrs. Molby and Mrs. Balmy happened the next night. Corah woke up once in the night and looked to see if the door had come back. It hadn't. So she went back to sleep. Nothing happened the next night either, or the next one.

But on the fourth night something did happen. Corah woke up when she thought she heard a whistle. She recognized the sound: it was Mr. Trilby's whistle, the one he used to summon the boat for Corah's first excursion. This could be interesting, she thought. So she jumped out of bed, put on some slippers and walked to the wall where the door had been. It wasn't there. Still she could hear Mr. Trilby's whistle. It came from the other side of the room. She turned and there it was. That same door with the dark brown wood panels that were like eyes.

"Here I am, over here!" Door winked one of its dark wood panels.

Corah walked over to the door and stood there looking at it. "Why are you there in this wall instead of over there in that wall where you were last time? And where is Mr. Trilby?"

"He's just on the other side of me. That's why I'm over here instead of over there."

"Now, Door. Wait just a minute," said Corah. "The boat dock is over there, not over here."

"He can put it anywhere he likes and this time he wants it over here. Besides, you heard his whistle."

Mr. Trilby blew his whistle again and this time it was clearly behind the door. "There!" said Door. "You hear that? Well, are you ready?"

"Ready for what? What's supposed to happen this time?"

"Oh well, that's for you to find out. Mr. Trilby will tell you more. So. Open me and go on in – or out, depending on how you look at it."

Corah thought about that a moment. "I'd say out," she decided.

"All right then. Out. Grab my gold door handle, open me and go on out."

"I'm not so sure," Corah mused. Then she added, "What's out there? What do the eyes on your backside see out there?

"Oh, I can tell you that. This time it's bright and sunny with puffy white clouds passing by. It's very nice. You'll like it."

"Bright and sunny!" Corah exclaimed. "It's the middle of the night!"

"Not on the other side of me." Then, by way of explanation, "Remember how the sun came out as you sailed to the island for tea?

Well, this time the sun is already out. See for yourself." And at that, Door opened itself.

Sure enough, the sun was bright enough on the other side to make Corah squint. She saw Mr. Trilby there wearing his bright red jacket with gold braids and the high crowned hat. She looked back at her dark bedroom and then at the sunny place beyond the door. "How do you do that?!"

"Actually, I don't do. That's just how it is. So stop dallying and get on with your excursion." With that, Door gently ushered her out onto the dock and closed itself behind her.

"About time you got here!" exclaimed Mr. Trilby. "Didn't you hear my whistle? I've been whistling for the past quarter hour. Any minute now I expect your conveyance to arrive and you have to be ready to go."

"Conveyance. What's a conveyance?" Corah wanted to know.

"Something that takes you places. In fact, here comes your conveyance now." He pointed up in the sky. It was something amazing. Coming slowly toward her was a weird flying machine that seemed to be floating in the air, making a buzzing sound. It looked like a bloated cigar or a loaf of bread, but it was really big. It had a little cabin with windows on its underside. It came buzzing closer and closer. Hanging from its front was a long rope.

"Oh dear!" cried Mr. Trilby. "I'm going to have to get the thing down here." Just when it was overhead, Mr. Trilby blew himself up into a round balloon (like he was when Corah first met him) and floated up to meet the thing. He grabbed the rope, punched his finger in his belly and, with a hissing sound, he shrank back to his normal size hauling the thing down to Corah's level. "There we are," he announced, wiping this brow.

"What is that thing?" she asked.

Trilby tied the rope to the dock and turned to Corah. "It's a blimp."

"Blimp? That's a funny word."

"Yes, and there's a funny little fellow who drives the blimp, but he can't always get it to stop. Don't worry, your excursion won't need a landing. You're going to visit a cloud where they play tennis."

"They play tennis on a cloud? You can't play tennis on a cloud. You can't even stand on a cloud. You'd slip through and fall to the ground."

"Not on our cloud. Just you wait and see. You do play tennis, don't you?"

"Not really. I can play soccer. Or T-ball. I'm pretty good at soccer."

"No, it's got to be tennis. Anything else and you'd fall right through the cloud. That's all right, though. You can just sit and watch. Lots of people are playing up there."

Out of the blimp's cabin jumped a little man with a tall tuft of hair on top of his head and fine, round potbelly. He wore a white knit shirt, white shorts, long white socks and white tennis shoes. He bounded over to Corah, saying, "Heigh ho! Name's Loblolly – Loblolly Joe. I got the name because of the tree they call loblolly because

I am so tall – tall as a tree." He stuck out his hand to Corah. Corah was surprised, first because of his appearance: he was barely taller than Corah and certainly nowhere near as tall as a tree. Second, she wasn't sure about the hand he stuck out in front of her. She thought he must want to shake hands, but when she tried to do it, he jerked his hand up and when she tried to reach it there, he dropped it down low and when she tried to reach it there, he swung around in a circle until he was facing her again. He put his hand in his pocket. "You can call me Joe or Lobby or Loll or Lollylob or Lowjoe, or whatever you like. Come on, get on board and I'll take you to a great cloud for tennis. They're already playing up there, you'll see. Come on!" He bounded back into the cabin. He put his head out one of the little windows, "Hey, let's go."

Mr. Trilby told Corah not to worry: "It'll be a great excursion."

Corah wasn't so sure. "Are you sure it's all right? I mean, he's a bit crazy."

"Oh, he's harmless and you'll get a kick out of him after a while. But I warn you he's voluble. He really is."

"Voluble? What's that? Is it dangerous?"

"Oh, no. It just means he talks a lot. You don't have to listen. It almost never means much of anything. Just watch the clouds out the little windows. They're beautiful this time of year."

Loblolly Joe came bounding back to Corah but when he got to her, he turned to Mr. Trilby, saying, "Hey, what's her name?"

Corah answered for herself, "I'm Corah."

"Is that Corah with an H or without one? See I'd pronounce it differently with the H. With the H, I'd say 'Corah' but without it, I'd say 'Cora.' You hear the difference?"

"It's with an H," said Mr. Trilby.

"OK, Corah, let's be on our way." And he went bounding back to the blimp cabin and got in.

Corah looked at Mr. Trilby, then at the blimp and back at Mr. Trilby, who said, "Go on. Have a good trip."

She sidled over to the cabin and got inside. It was like being in a little room with a low ceiling and lots of little square windows all around. Loblolly Joe leaned out one of the windows and called out, "Untie the rope, Trilby." Mr. Trilby did. The blimp rose up in the air and the buzzing sound started up again. As it flew gently into the clouds, Corah looked down and she could see her house on Parkview Avenue and the whole park next to the house with its trails and lakes. It all seemed dark as night down there but up above the sky was bright and blue. The blimp suddenly went right into a cloud and out the windows everything was blank and bright white.

That instant, Loblolly Joe started talking and he went on talking, and on and on and on, even after the blimp came out the top of the cloud. He talked about clouds, and how some of them were thick and some were thin. Some you could glide right into and out of but others you could jump up and down on and play games. "You have to know the difference," he said and went on, "We're going to one of the specially numbered clouds – those are the safe ones for jumping on. And the numbered clouds, they all have little flags on them, like that one over there. See? That flag shows number four. That's Cloud Four. See? Cloud Four isn't nearly as good for games as Cloud Eight and that's why we're flying to Cloud Eight. See?"

Corah nodded her head to show she understood and he wouldn't have to go on talking. But he did anyway. "See, when we get to Cloud Eight there'll be lots of people there, all playing tennis. Oh, it's great to see them playing tennis together, all over the cloud. You can play too, if you want. You do play tennis, don't you?" He didn't wait for an answer; besides she already answered that question. He talked about the game of tennis and how wonderful it was.

Corah quit listening. She was much more interested in the shapes of the clouds that were passing by. Some were beautiful, piling billowy white shapes on top of one another so they towered high into the sky. Then she saw a flat cloud and on it a flag that showed the number eight. "There it is!" she cried.

"What?" Loblolly Joe blurted out. He hadn't been paying attention.

"Cloud Eight! There it is!"

"Oh." Loblolly banked the blimp to the right and settled it into the top mist of Cloud Eight. Corah looked out one of the little cabin windows. Cloud Eight was crowded with Loblolly-like little people everywhere she looked. They were all just as short as Loblolly Joe and they all had the tall tufts of hair standing out on top of their heads and they had fine potbellies and they all wore identical white knit shirts and white shorts and white socks and white tennis shoes. And they were all hitting white tennis balls this way and that with their racquets – and yet none of the balls fell off the cloud. Instead they came right back to the persons who hit them after bouncing in the top mist of the cloud. There weren't any marks to make a court, but there were people perched on high chairs. They were all shouting words like, "Ad in, deuce, love forty, game point, let, fault," and so on. It didn't make much sense to Corah. The people went right on whacking balls with their racquets.

Corah by now was out of the cabin and standing in the top mist on Cloud Eight. Loblolly Joe jumped out of the cabin with a racquet and ball that he brought right to Corah. "Here, hold the racquet in one hand and the ball in the other, then throw the ball straight up in the air and smack it a good one with the racquet. When the ball goes out, it'll bounce in the mist and then turn around, bounce again and come back to you and then you can smack it again and it'll go out and come back. See?"

Corah said she saw and threw the ball up and smacked it hard. When it came back, she gave it another whack and out it went again. It was really fun. She kept doing it until the little man nearest her in his high chair shouted "Game over! Change sides!" Well, there weren't any sides; there wasn't even a net. People caught their balls coming back and then just turned around, faced the opposite direction and went right on smacking the tennis balls.

When Corah turned around she suddenly became aware that Loblolly Joe wasn't there any more. He had disappeared in the crowd. How could she ever find him again? He looked just like everyone else. The place was huge and he could be anywhere. Now she was worried. What if she didn't get home and back in bed before her mother would call her to get up for school? "Where is he?" she said to herself. She went from one person to the next asking if they knew Loblolly Joe and where he was. No one knew.

Finally, one of those funny little people asked, "Why do you want to find this Loblolly fellow?"

"He's supposed to take me home in the blimp."

"What blimp?"

She looked around. The blimp was gone. Now she was really worried. She was on the verge of tears. The little person said, "It's all right. I know just what to do." He pulled out a very large umbrella. Look, take this umbrella and follow me." They went together to the edge of the cloud. When Corah looked down she could just make out the dock with Mr. Trilby standing there. "See, that's where you want to go. We're right above your place. So all you have to do is open the umbrella and step out and you'll float slowly and quietly down, see?"

"Are you sure?" Corah had to ask as she opened the umbrella.

"Sure I am. Look, I'll hold your hand and you try it." So she took his hand and stepped out, and sure enough she was out there floating. "You all right now?" She said, "Yes," very relieved. He let go of her hand and she floated down ever so slowly until she was standing next to Mr. Trilby on the dock. It was wonderful to float in the air like that.

"Ah, there you are! But where's Loblolly Joe and his blimp?"

Corah folded up the magical umbrella and handed it to Mr. Trilby saying, "I don't know! He disappeared and so did his blimp. Lucky thing I got this magical umbrella or I'd still be up there on Cloud Eight."

"Aha!" said Trilby. "That explains it all. Any time he gets anywhere near Cloud Nine he can't wait to get on it. No matter what he might be doing he'll drop it just to be on Cloud Nine."

"What's so special about Cloud Nine?"

"Well, I don't actually know. I've never been there, but everyone says just being there makes people happy." Mr. Trilby folded up the magical umbrella..

Just then Door opened itself saying, "Welcome back, Corah. You must be tired. Are you ready to get back to bed. "

"Yes, but actually I had a wonderful time playing tennis, riding in a blimp and floating under an umbrella." She went in, took off her slippers and got back in bed and slept all through the night.

When she woke the next morning, her mother was at the door. "Did you sleep well, dear?"

"Oh yes," she replied, "I had a wonderful time."

"That's a funny thing to say about your sleep."

It really was a funny thing to say about sleep, but Corah decided not to explain. She got out of bed and got dressed to go to school.

Excursion #3:

"Off to the Races Under the Sea"

For several nights in a row there had been no sounds in the night. Corah woke up two or three times each night to see if the door had come back in her room, but it was never there. She thought she might not have any more magical excursions in the night. That made her sad. She liked those excursions. She wanted to share them with her little sister, Sienna. She never told her about them and she wanted to surprise her the next time. It would be fun to surprise her. But she guessed it wouldn't happen. At least she slept better after that.

That is until she woke one night when she heard a gurgling sound. At first she decided there was no sound, but then she heard it again, louder. Something *was* making a gurgling sound. She sat bolt upright in bed. The door was there again! She jumped out of bed and ran to the door. Door looked right at her and winked one eye. "Ready?" it asked.

"Where am I going?"

"Oh, you're going to like this one. I can tell you that."

"You can tell me more than that." Corah insisted.

"Oh, all right. You're going on an underwater adventure this time. Now, are you ready?"

"No. I can't go underwater dressed like this! And how am I supposed to breathe underwater?"

"Oh, that's all taken care of. It's all magical – you won't even get wet! Now, are you ready?"

"No. I want my sister to come with me this time. I want her to know what these trips in the night are like. Don't worry about her – she knows how to behave. I'll go wake her up then you can open yourself and let us out. All right?"

"No, no, no! You can't wake her up. Nobody goes on magical excursions in the night if they're awake. You got that? Nobody!"

"What do you mean? Here I am. I'm awake."

"No, you're not. You just think you are."

"I'm not awake?"

"No, you're not. Look!"

And Corah turned and looked at her bed. There she was! She saw herself sound asleep in her bed. She was amazed. How could she be in two places at once? She turned back to the door. "You mean I am really over there in bed and not here at all?"

"Well no. You're here all right. Your dreaming mind put you here. So long as you're sleeping over there, you'll be on this excursion over here."

That puzzled Corah. "That doesn't make any sense. You're saying I can go on excursions only if I'm asleep and my sister Sienna can't come if she's awake."

"Right!" said Door.

"Well, can't you do something so she could come along? Get her dreaming mind to put her here? How about that? You could do that, couldn't you?"

"No, actually, I couldn't. I suppose Mr. Trilby could. I don't know. Tell you what. I'll ask him. He's just there on the other side of me."

With that, Door went blank. Its eyes and mouth disappeared. Corah could hear some muttering going on outside the door. After a while Door's eyes and mouth came back around. Door looked pleased and announced, "Mr. Trilby said he'd take care of it. You'll see."

All at once there was Sienna standing right next to her sister. She looked up at Corah and then at the door. "How'd I get here? And what's that gurgling sound?"

"You're going on an excursion with me. Isn't that great?"

"What's an excursion?" Sienna wasn't sure about any of this.

"It's a kind of trip, see? We go places."

"Is it going to be okay?"

"More than okay. It'll be great. You'll see. I went on two excursions already, once in a boat and once in a blimp. I want you to come along and they said it'd be all right. We'll have fun."

Sienna was doubtful. "What's a blimp?"

"It's like a flying balloon. But it doesn't matter. This time we're going underwater. Isn't that right, Door?"

Sienna looked up and saw the door was looking at her. She was startled. "Is that door watching me?" she wanted to know.

"Well, yes. And it'll talk to you, too – tell us about our excursion if you just be quiet."

"Okay, but this is really weird."

Door harrumphed. "If you two are through jabbering, I'll tell you about this excursion. Now you heard some gurgling, right? It's coming from a submarine ball that's waiting to take you underwater. Mr. Trilby is about to tie it up at the dock. You ready for it?"

"Oh, yeah. We're ready, aren't we Sienna?" Corah looked right at Sienna who just looked back.

The door flung itself open and the two sisters, holding hands, walked slowly through and out onto the dock. There they saw Mr. Trilby. He was pulling on a chain that went over a bunch of pulleys. Out of the water rose a big, strange round iron ball. It had a large round window on its side. When he got it up right next to the dock, he tied down the chain and then turned to the two girls. "About time you got here," he said. "Now who is this who's coming along with you?"

"Thank you, Miss Corah. Very nicely done. Pleased to meet you, Sienna, I'm sure. Yes, tour director, that's me. Now tonight, you're going to the races down under the sea. This marvelous contraption will take you there. I call it a bathysphere. It can take you way down deep. Allow me to open this round window – it's also a door. There's a fellow inside who will explain the whole plan to you." The door opened and out stepped a little man dressed in a colorful costume like jockeys wear. He even had a crop in his hand.

"That's my sister, Sienna. I want her to come along on this excursion." Then Corah remembered her manners: "Sienna, this is Mr. Trilby. He's our tour director. He makes our trips happen, see? Where are we going tonight, Mr. Trilby?"

Corah knew that was what jockeys wear when they race horses. But this is confusing. "Are you a horse jockey?" she asked at once.

"Right-O," said the little man. "We gonna rightch way to da races. How 'bout dat? Innit wunnerful?"

"What kind of races?" Sienna wanted to know, because she was still a little suspicious.

"Da horse races, acourse," said the little man.

"What kind of horses can race under the sea?" Now Corah was skeptical.

"Why, sea horses, acourse."

That almost made Corah and Sienna laugh out loud, but Mr. Trilby interrupted and did the introductions: "This is Corah and her sister Sienna and this is Weydon Undersey."

"Glada meetcha."

"He's got a kind of funny face," whispered Sienna. It was true. His face, his whole head, was like a fish head. He had gills but he also had nostrils.

Mr. Trilby was quick to explain: "You see, Mr. Undersey is a special sort and he can get air from his gills or his nostrils. Most sea horse jockeys are like him. He has a funny way of talking too, but you'll get used to it and understand him just fine. He's going to take you down in the bathysphere and you'll see all kinds of swimming

creatures through that round window. Then he'll stop and let you get on your very own sea horses and ride them to the race. Mr. Undersey is going to be in the race. You can cheer him on. Maybe he'll win." Mr. Trilby opened the round window-door, saying, "You better be on your way. Don't want to be late."

Corah and Sienna stepped in, looking all around that strange contraption. Mr. Undersey jumped in, turned around and spun a wheel that locked the door. Then he sat at the controls, pulled a lever and pushed a button, and the ball sank right into the water, traveling faster and faster. Corah and Sienna watched out the window and saw lots of bright colored fish darting this way and that.

"Now, cumin up reel soon you gonna see a big okkipus," Mr. Undersey announced, and sure enough there right in front of the window was a huge octopus waving its eight tentacles. The girls were amazed What was even more amazing was a great whale that stopped and looked right in the window at them and then swam away. Mr. Undersey declared, "Didja see dat? Wunnit wunnerful, eh?" Corah and Sienna agreed it really was wonderful.

"Goils, you gotcha do sumpin before you can get out wid da horses, okay? Der's magic blue stuff dat'll keep youse dry and letcha breathe even dough youse in da water. I got some for eacha youse. Here. Drink it up, okay?" And he took a pitcher and two glasses and poured the blue stuff into each glass. It tasted pretty good, something like blueberries. Mr. Undersey took back the glasses and turned to the controls. He made the bathysphere slow down and settle into a place where a group of sea horses were corralled. Mr. Undersey jumped up, twirled the wheel that opened the round window-door and bounded out of the bathysphere. The girls held back a little, afraid of going out into the water even if they did drink the magic blue stuff. They came out and they really could breathe and their clothes stayed perfectly dry. They looked around and saw five or six other jockeys who greeted Mr. Undersey. Actually they all looked alike with the same fish heads. The only difference was the color of their costumes. They all seemed like friends. Then Mr. Undersey brought two sea horses to the girls. Each one had a saddle, a bit and a rein. Mr. Undersey helped Corah and Sienna into the saddles. They trotted their sea horses around a little to get a feel for riding them.

When Mr. Undersey jumped on his own horse, all three of them galloped off together. The horses were very fast. They even made the girls feel what seemed like wind in their hair as they rode along. Mr. Undersey was talking but they couldn't quite make out what he was saying. It was something about the racetrack and how he was going to be in the race. What was fun was getting the horses to gallop right and left, up and down, faster and slower. Suddenly Mr. Undersey wasn't in front of them anymore. He had disappeared. They pulled on their reins and came to an abrupt stop. They looked all around. Corah called out his name. A voice came from way down below them: "Da racetrack's dis way. Come on." So they turned the horses down and joined Mr. Undersey who greeted them "How 'bout dat ride? Wunnit wunnerful?" They agreed that it was wonderful.

Soon they came to a grandstand at the edge of the track. There were all sorts of sea creatures floating about in the grandstand:

Tuna, dolphins, sea turtles, sharks, a couple of squids, some giant lobsters, all of them shouting and calling out the names of their favorite horses. They were funny names: Happy Bounder, Right-of-Way, Precious Gait, All-Over-Good, and so on.

Corah turned to Mr. Undersey and asked him what his horse's name was. He replied "Late Start."

"Why do you call him that?" Corah wanted to know.

"It's 'cause he allus starts late, den he pours it on and passes all de udders. You two gocha take yer places 'count the race 'bouta start. I gocha get dunn to da startin' gate. See youse laita, okay? It gonna be wunnerful." With that, Mr. Undersey trotted off. Corah and Sienna tied up their horses and found a place next to a walrus with a moustache that reminded them of Mr. Trilby.

Down on the track a blowfish sounded a trumpet and the loudspeaker voice rattled off the names and the numbers of the horses already lined up at the starting gate. Late Start was number 9. Corah thought that might be lucky, like Cloud 9. The blowfish made a popping noise and the horses were off. Late Start was true to his name, holding back from the crowd. Corah and Sienna started shouting at him: "Come on, Late Start! Go, go, go!" Late Start seemed to hear them. At any rate, he started picking up speed and soon he was up with the crowd. After a while he even passed the crowd. Then he was in the lead just barely ahead of Precious Gait. And the two battled it out, one with a nose ahead and then the other. They came to the finish line and it was Late Start by a nose! The crowd went wild and Corah and Sienna jumped up and down shouting the name of their favorite horse. They ran down to the winner's circle and patted Late Start on the nose. They congratulated Mr. Undersey and they all smiled happily. And of course Mr. Undersey declared, "How 'bout dat? Wunnit wunnerful?"

Late Start had a garland of flowers around his neck and Mr. Undersey had a trophy as they all went back to the corral where the bathysphere was waiting to take them home. This time they all rode along slowly but happily. When they got to the corral, Mr. Undersey put the horses away in the corral after giving them some sea oats to eat and some good seawater to drink. Then he opened the round window-door and all three got in.

The trip back to the dock went well and they saw some more strange fish, ones with fancy flashing lights that lit up all the surroundings. Then they felt a tug and they saw Mr. Trilby pulling the bathysphere up out of the water. The round window-door opened. Corah and Sienna stepped out. They turned back and thanked Mr. Undersey, who, of course, enthused, "How 'bout dat? Wunnit wunnerful?" And they of course agreed. The window-door closed and the bathysphere sank back into the water.

Mr. Trilby said that he was glad they had such a good time, but that it was probably time for them to get back into their beds. So he told Door to open up. Door welcomed them home and flung itself open. Once inside and after Door closed, the two sisters looked at each other. Sienna said, "How 'bout dat?" And Corah said, "Wunnit wunnerful?" They laughed and went to bed.

The next morning Sienna looked at Corah and asked, "Did you dream last night about being underwater?' And Corah replied, "Yes, but it's our secret. Right?' Sienna agreed, "Yeah. Our secret excursion."

Excursion #4:

"In Search of the Unicorn"

THE WIND OUTSIDE OF CORAH'S BEDROOM MADE A whistling sound in the trees and sometimes something seemed to knock against the wall making a TAP-TAP sound. Corah had trouble sleeping. It all sounded a little scary. Actually she did fall asleep without knowing it only then to sit up and look around the room. In the dark she could just make out the door, that door that was there only when it was time for an excursion. She got out of bed and tiptoed across the room to the door. It was rattling against the wind making that tap-tap sound. Door had its eyes clinched shut and its mouth was tightly turned down.

"Hey, Door! Is something wrong?"

Slowly Door opened its eyes and looked at Corah. "Oh, no, nothing. Nothing, nothing. Nothing is wrong. Everything is just fine."

"You want me to open you?"

"Well, of course you can do that. I mean that's what my handle is for. I can't stop you, but I can tell you there is something scary out there. It's not just the wind. You might not like it. Maybe you ought to go back to bed."

Corah could hear Mr. Trilby's whistle. He always blew his whistle once he had the next excursion ready. That meant that he wanted Corah to come out onto the dock. Corah felt puzzled. Door had

never before been so nervous and Mr. Trilby seemed very insistent blowing the whistle so loudly. She thought about this and finally she made up her mind: "I am going to open you, Door, and I am going to find what this is all about."

"All right, if you insist, but don't forget I warned you." Door closed its eyes tight shut as Corah reached out and turned the handle. The wind blew the door all the way open and there on the other side was Mr. Trilby, still blowing his whistle so hard his eyes popped.

Corah was a little annoyed and she blurted out, "That's enough, Mr. Trilby. I'm here now."

"Ah there you are! I have been blowing up a storm trying to get you out here. I guess I was hard to hear. Look, I have a wonderful excursion for you, but it is a little scary. Are you ready for something scary?"

'Well, that depends. Is there something dangerous out there?"

Just then Corah herd a loud snort right behind her. She whirled around and saw a huge creature looking at her with sharp, penetrating eyes. Corah nearly jumped out of her skin! This beast had the head and front legs of an eagle and the body of a lion. It also had great spreading feathered wings. Mr. Trilby put out his hand to Corah who ran to him. She was really scared.

"Now, now. No need to be afraid. This is a griffin. I admit he's

awfully big, but he'll be your friend and fly you where you need to go tonight. Isn't that right, Gregory? That's his name, you see: Gregory the griffin."

Corah looked up at the gigantic beast feeling just a little unsure about this excursion that Mr. Trilby has planned. The griffin bowed his great head and than said something that sounded like "Awr kip yer saff, dunner werry."

Mr. Trilby felt moved to explain: "He has trouble speaking clearly because of that sharp beak of his. He just said he'll keep you safe, don't you worry."

"Now I really don't like this." And with that, Corah walked back to Door, which by now had managed to close itself. She stopped short when the griffin whimpered, "Yer dunna breev mee?" And Gregory the griffin looked sad. Corah thought he looked very sad.

Mr. Trilby, however, was looking stern. "Now, see here, Corah. Who was it said she really wanted to see a unicorn?"

"Me." Corah had to admit it.

"And who is the tour director here?"

"You are."

"And suppose I, as tour director, tell you that the only way to see a unicorn is to fly off on the back of a griffin. He has come a long way just to help us out. Do you want to send him away after all that?"

"Where is he going to take me?"

"Ah well." Mr. Trilby seemed to hesitate a little. "First he'll fly straight to the deep and dark Woobah Wood. Then he'll walk you through the woods and out the other side. And then he'll take you across Sinkhole Plain all the way to the labyrinth and so on."

"What do you mean 'and so on?' And what's a labyrinth, anyway? This really sounds pretty scary."

Mr. Trilby held up his fore finger. "Oh, I didn't tell you about the Voice. That makes all the difference. Yes, the Voice. Just listen to the Voice and do what it says to do and you'll do fine even when there's danger."

"Voice? What voice? I don't hear any voice."

"That Voice!" And Mr. Trilby held up his fore finger again. Out of nowhere, but maybe just overhead, came these words: "Do not be afraid. I will be with you."

"Who said that?"

"It's just the Voice. It will be with you for the whole excursion."

Corah thought that was strange, but it was also a real comfort. Then she looked at the griffin who tipped his head as if to encourage her. She really would like to see that unicorn. "Well, okay. But it still sounds scary. I want to take my little dog with me. I'd feel better with my dog Odin along."

With that Corah went to Door who was still rattling even if the wind had died down quite a bit. As she opened it to go inside, it muttered, "I hope you know what you're doing." Inside Corah called for Odin (very quietly so as not to wake anyone) "Odie, Odie, Odie!" Then she realized that she would have to get him out of his crate. So she tiptoed down to his crate and picked him up. When she carried Odin out onto the dock, Mr. Trilby was showing the griffin a map of tonight's excursion. It looked like this:

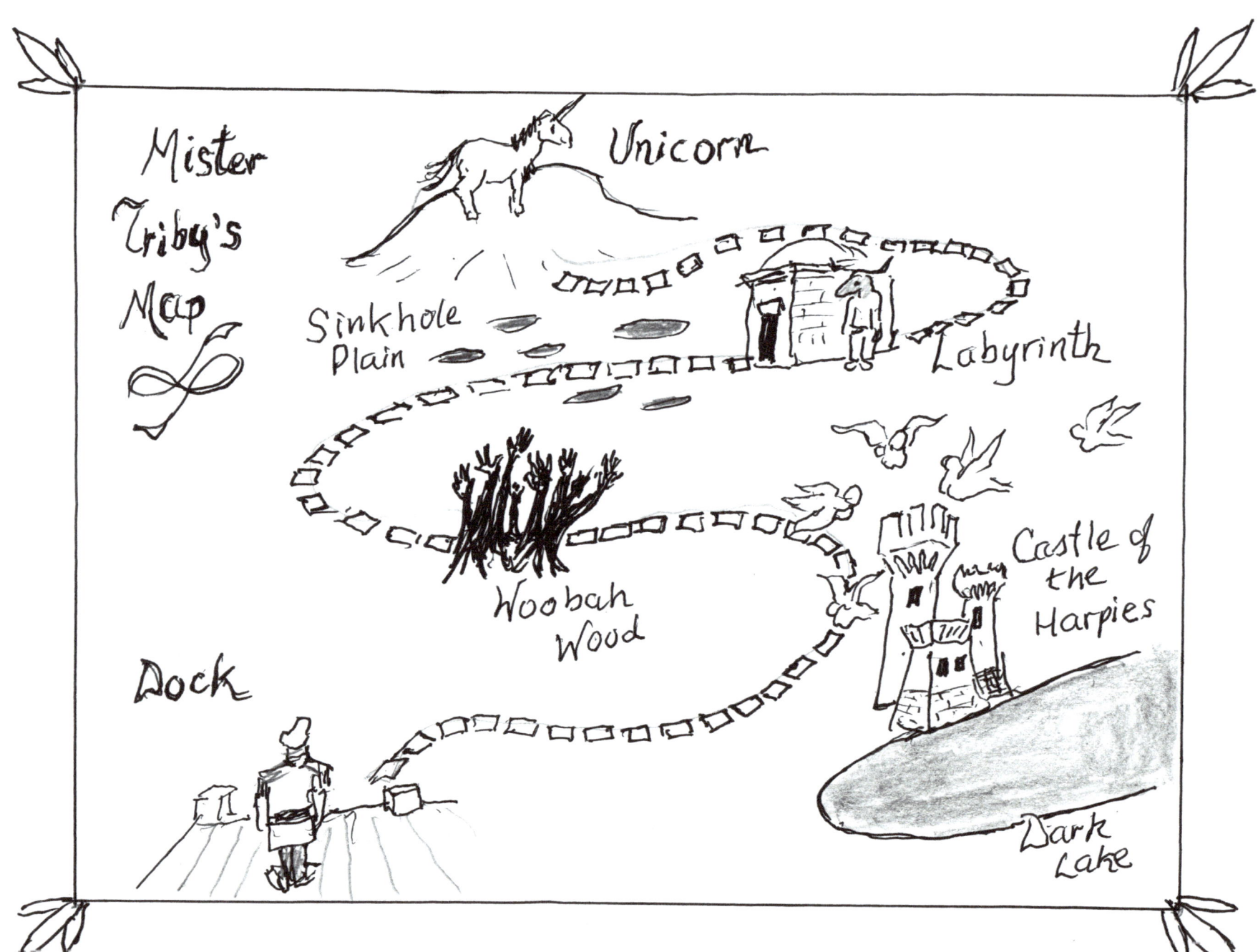

Mister Triby's Map

Unicorn

Sinkhole Plain

Labyrinth

Woobah Wood

Castle of the Harpies

Dock

Dark Lake

It showed the gnarled, grasping trees of Woobah Wood, the boiling pits on Sinkhole Plains, the twisting passages of the labyrinth and the sunny hill of the unicorn. The map did make things look really scary, but the Voice spoke again out of nowhere: "Do not be afraid. I will be with you." Odin heard that and made a few little barks that seemed to say, "ME TOO!"

Corah turned to the griffin. "How are we supposed to get on top of this animal?" As if he understood, Gregory the griffin went down on his knees and spread one of his great wings out along the ground. That made a sort of ladder for Corah and Odin to climb up onto the griffin's back. Once they were up there, Gregory the griffin stood up and spread both wings. Mr. Trilby saluted and shouted, "Have a great trip both of you – er, all three of you!" And, here the moon was scudding among the clouds. Down below they could see towns with their lights flickering in the night, and then hills, valleys and a large, dark lake. At the edge of the lake was a castle perched on a cliff with towers and turrets and ramparts. Inside it was all lit up and they could hear music and laughter. All of a sudden a swarm of little flying creatures flew at the griffin. They were very strange. Each had with the head and body of a woman but the wings, tail feathers and feet of a bird. They all were screeching words that sounded like "Eeeecome, come. comeeee with us. Comeeee Fun. Come

down eeee." But the Voice said, "Don't. If you go down there you'll be trapped and you'll never get out and never go home again." Odin looked ferociously at them and made a growl deep in his throat. Gregory the griffin understood and flew out of the range of the screeching creatures.

They flew high in the sky where the moon was scudding among the clouds. Down below they could see towns with their lights flickering in the night, and then hills, valleys and a large, dark lake. At the edge of the lake was a castle perched on a cliff with towers and turrets and ramparts. Inside it was all lit up and they could hear music and laughter. All of a sudden a swarm of little flying creatures flew at the griffin. They were very strange. Each had with the head and body of a woman but the wings, tail feathers and feet of a bird. They all were screeching words that sounded like "Eeeecome, come. comeeee with us. Comeeee Fun. Come down eeee." But the Voice said, "Don't. If you go down there you'll be trapped and you'll never get out and never go home again." Odin looked ferociously at them and made a growl deep in his throat. Gregory the griffin understood and flew out of the range of the screeching creatures.

Corah held him tightly as they flew on into the night. Not knowing where the Voice was, she looked up and said, "What were those screaming creatures? I've never seen anything like them." The Voice answered from her left side, saying, "They're miniature harpies. They're dangerous if you ever accept any invitation from them. What sounded like laughter was really screaming for help."

Corah was glad to leave them behind but just then the griffin swooped down to the ground. When he stopped Corah and Odin looked ahead. They were in front of a snarl of trees, their naked limbs waving about wildly although the wind was gone now and the air quiet. The limbs seemed to have long, long fingers and they started grasping for Corah and Odin.

The Voice spoke as Corah hoped it would, this time from her right side: "Be very careful. These are the grasping trees of the Woo-bah Wood. Don't let them touch you or they'll grapple you into their trunks."

"I don't want to go in there. Let's just fly over all those trees. Why can't we do that?" That would make sense to Corah.

"Two reasons," the Voice explained. "One, the trees kick up so much disturbance in the air that Gregory the griffin can lose his bearings and fall into the wood. Two, nobody can get to the unicorn who has not shown the courage it takes to go through Woobah Wood." The Voice then gave Gregory the griffin directions and he nodded to show that he understood and he started into the wood.

All along the Voice was saying, "Keep to the right, go left, now right again." Suddenly a tree thrust its limb out within inches of the griffin, who nimbly skirted around the tree. That happened again and again. Those gnarled limbs seemed to be everywhere and they made creaking noises every time they moved. Odin growled and Corah sometimes covered her eyes, but the Voice kept on guiding them. Then all at once there was no more noise and Corah looked up and saw that they were out of the woods. Not one branch had touched them. What a relief it was! And Odin made a little bark that sounded like "Okay!"

But now ahead of them in the semi-darkness was a flat land, a large field that looked as though it went on beyond the horizon. Corah noticed something peculiar about the field: every once in a while she heard a burp and then she saw a big hole open up. There were holes all over the field and more kept appearing with those peculiar burps. This had to be the Sinkhole Plain. It would really be bad to have the earth drop out from under you if you were in the wrong place at the wrong time. To make things worse, the sinkholes were boiling, making burp sounds and a lot of steam. Half to herself Corah said, "I don't want to go out there. Let's just go home."

The Voice spoke soothingly, this time from somewhere overhead, saying, "Do not be afraid. I will be with you. I will guide Gregory the griffin around all the sinkholes. We're going to find that unicorn." With that, the Voice started giving directions: straight ahead for twenty-five yards, angle to the right for ten yards, now hard left for fifteen yards, and so on and so on. Gregory did just as the Voice said. They passed boiling holes and sometimes they just avoided a sudden spurt of hot steaming water. Corah and Odin held on tight because they jumped every time the ground fell nearby or a fountain of hot water blew up in front of them.

They came out on the other side of Sinkhole Plain and before they could catch their breath a great wall rose up in front of them blocking their path. The wall towered over them. There was a door. Written on the door were the words: "Labyrinth. Beware of Minotaur." Corah held Odin tightly against her chest. There was no way around the wall and going back through Sinkhole Plain was out of the question. She gulped and then blurted out, "Now what?" For the moment the Voice was silent.

Gregory the griffin said in his usual hoarse voice, "Ar haffa go naw." Saying that, he knelt down and spread his wing out for Corah and Odin to slide down. "What?!" said Corah. "Did you say you have to go now? You're leaving us here?"

"He has to," explained the Voice at last. He has to carried you through the Woobah Wood and across Sinkhole Plain but he is much too big to go into the labyrinth. We have to let him go back to his home." Corah and Odin slid down the griffin's wing. She wanted to give Gregory a hug, but it is not easy to hug a griffin. So she just said, "Thank you, Gregory. You are a great griffin." Gregory replied shyly, "Yerelcum." Then he stood up, spread both wings, and took off flying toward the moon.

That left Corah and Odin at a loss standing at that door. In a few moments, they heard the Voice say, "I'm still here." Corah was glad to hear that, but she was bothered about this thing called a labyrinth. If she has to go in there it would be useful to know what it is. "What is a labyrinth anyway?"

"It is a maze of passageways. They go this way and that and some of them end with a blank wall and you have to go back. You can really get lost in there, but if you manage to make the right turns you will find your way out. But if not, you can be trapped. So you don't want to make too many wrong turns. That's why I am with you."

"Wait, wait! What's this Minotaur we're supposed to beware of? Is it dangerous?"

"Oh, yes, the Minotaur! He's dangerous all right. He even looks dangerous. He has a huge man's body and the head of a great bull. But worse than that, they say he eats people, especially young people. So, yes, he's dangerous. Don't worry. I'll be with you."

Up to now, Corah had faith in the Voice, but this time she was not so sure. She turned and saw that the door was opening of its own accord and inside were three passageways, one leading straight ahead and the other two to the sides. Odin made a bark that seemed to say, "Watch out – here I come."

The Voice went a little ahead, saying, "Look for some string on the ground. A fellow named Theseus left it there to help him get out a long time ago. He also claimed he killed the Minotaur, but maybe he was just saying that. So be alert." They followed the string as it turned into one passageway after another. They went left, then right, then left again, the Voice still guiding them. But all of a sudden, they turned one corner and there was the Minotaur looming over them. Corah and Odin froze (although Odin did manage a little growl.) "Oh, dear!" said the Voice.

Corah looked up to where she thought the Voice might be. She thought to herself, "It's all very well for the Voice. The Minotaur can't see the Voice." And the Minotaur's great bull head made him seem powerful enough to eat little people and creatures such as dogs. He was staring down at Corah and Odin. They took a couple of steps back until they banged into a wall. Odin made the most ferocious bark he could bark. This was really scary.

But then a strange thing happened. That great beast, the Minotaur, with his bull's head staring down on the two shaking beings, spoke five words in a quiet gentle tone: "I want to be friends." Corah and Odin were so startled they sat down right then and there. The Minotaur did the same thing and the three sat there looking at each other. For some little while they sat there like that. The Minotaur spoke again in that same quiet gentle tone: "I've been hoping someone would come along. It's awfully lonely living in a labyrinth. No one ever comes to visit. They're afraid they won't get out."

Corah almost choked with relief. "I bet they are afraid of you, Mr. Minotaur. That's why they don't come."

"Yes, but you see I'm not so scary, am I?"

"No, you're not," said the Voice.

"Who said that?" asked the Minotaur.

"It's our friend Voice who leads us through all dangers."

"Oh." said the Minotaur. "Thank you, Voice, for bringing these visitors to me. People don't come because of lies that Theseus told about me. He was the one who told everyone that I ate people, especially young people. It's not true. He also boasted that he killed me. But he didn't. I don't look killed, do I?"

No, no, not at all!" said Corah and Odin barked three short barks that sounded like "NOPE, NOPE, NOPE."

The Voice declared that it knew all along that Theseus had lied

41

about the Minotaur. "But he really did lay down that string in the passageways."

"I tell you what. Since you're here, let me show you around my place. After that I'll show you the way out. Okay?" The Minotaur stood up and motioned for them to follow him. He took them into beautiful chambers and halls all lit with candles in candelabras. There were paintings and tapestries on the walls and fine furniture everywhere. The Minotaur had a palace deep inside the labyrinth, a palace no one knew about. The Voice remarked that people have been telling awful lies about him for years, for centuries.

They then came to a fine, decorated door and the Minotaur announced, "This is your way out. When you have the chance, please tell people what the Minotaur is really like."

"We surely will," said the Voice.

"YEP, YEP, YEP," said Odin.

"You're no people-eater. That Theseus guy ought to pay for all the lies he told." That was Corah's opinion.

They stepped through the door and out into the open. There in front of them was a beautiful hillside with the dawning sun just beginning to make it sparkle. Corah and Odin stood there gazing up at the steep hill. Quietly, the Vice said, "It is beautiful isn't it?" For a few moments the three of tem stood transfixed. Then the Voice

announced, "And now I'll take you to the top of this hill and there you will find that unicorn we been searching for."

So they set out. The higher they climbed on the hill the brighter the sun became. A warm breeze gave them comfort. When they reached the top of the hill, they were at the edge of a meadow and in the middle of that meadow, glowing white in the sun, stood the unicorn. It was a beautiful vision no one could ever describe. Corah and Odin stood stock still staring in wonder.

The unicorn slowly stepped toward them. The sunlight glinted off the golden horn as the animal knelt down in front of Corah. In deep wonder, she reached out her hand to touch the unicorn's forehead.

42

"Now," the Voice said, "if you will get on the unicorn, she and I will see you home. She will gallop through the day and back into last night when you got on Gregory the griffin."

Corah and Odin got up on the unicorn who then stood up, turned and began to walk, then trot and finally gallop. They were on their way back to Mr. Trilby's dock. The Voice gave directions in a tone so soft that after a while it lulled Corah and Odin off to sleep as they rode gently across the land.

Back at the dock, Mr. Trilby called out a welcome and blew his whistle. Corah and Odin opened their eyes and saw where they were. The unicorn came to rest and let Corah and Odin down. Corah patted the unicorn's nose in thanks. Then the unicorn stood up and nodded as if to say, "Pleased to help." Corah watched in wonder as it turned and trotted off in graceful dignity. She turned to Mr. Trilby and said, "That was not just an excursion. It was an adventure." He smiled as if to say that he knew it would be. Looking around, Corah said, "Voice, wherever you are, thank you. I would never have gotten through all those dangers without you." Now the Voice seemed far up in the air as it called out, "We did it together and I was always with you. Sleep tight!" And the Voice seemed to fade away in the air overhead. Corah and Odin went to Door, who was glad to see them safely back home.

Once inside, Corah took Odin back to his crate. They sat there for just a while thinking about the scary things they had met on the excursion. Corah wanted to know if Odin was ever really frightened, and Odin sort of replied with a sound deep in his throat as if to say, "Well, maybe a little." Corah agreed, and she added, "I was glad you were there with me." And Odin made another sound, this one a proud but quiet bark that seemed to say, "I was there for you." She kissed him on the nose and opened the crate for him to go in. He settled down on his bed and she closed the gate.

Corah went to her bed and was soon falling back to sleep. She stopped for a moment and looked for the door and saw that it had disappeared. She smiled to herself and settled back down for a good night's sleep full of memories of the Voice, Gregory the griffin, the Minotaur and --best of all – the beautiful unicorn.

Excu on #5:

"A Place for Ideas and Stories and Pictures"

*I*T HAD BEEN MANY NIGHTS SINCE CORAH'S LAST EX-cursion, the one that took her to the unicorn. Now to-night she was feeling restless. She tossed and turned in her bed wanting to get to sleep and hoping to see that door to Trilby's dock appear. That would mean a new excursion. But she knew that she had to be deeply asleep for that to happen. The door never appeared unless she was asleep; then her dream mind would pick her up and take her to the door.

Something else was on Corah's mind. She wanted to write a story about people bouncing on pogo sticks but she was stuck. She couldn't figure out where she should take the story. It had to be something to do with how people used the pogo sticks. Somebody told her she should sleep on it. Perhaps then the idea would come to her. That was another reason she wanted to get to sleep.

While she was thinking these things, she must have fallen to sleep because the next thing she knew she was putting on her slip-pers and walking over to where the door appeared last time. She was saying to herself that Mr. Trilby might help her with her pogo stick story. Maybe he could fix up an excursion just for that purpose. She stood staring at that wall. She gave it an intense stare. It was so strong that the door very slowly began to appear. At first it was faint and then more and more vivid until it was all there. But the eyes in the two upper panels were still shut.

"Hey, Door!' Corah said loudly. "Wake up!"

Door opened its eyes slowly and turned them to look at Corah. "What in the world do you want?"

Corah was quick to answer: "I want an excursion to a place where ideas become stories and pictures." She knew exactly what she wanted.

"Wait just a minute. You don't announce excursions. Mr. Trilby does that. He's the only one. And then he lets me know it's time to appear. And it's not that time now. You understand?" With that, Door began to close its eyes.

"Don't you go back to sleep. Tell Mr. Trilby I'm here."

Door sighed. "I don't know if I can do that. Right now he's probably puffed himself up floating around out there as he always does between excursions. What's more, I don't think there is any such place."

"If anyone knows about that, it would be Mr. Trilby. Let me open you and go ask him. Maybe I can bring him down and we could talk."

"This is a fine howdy-do! You've got some nerve I must say. Who-ever heard of such a thing – you demanding your very own excur-sion? Mr. Trilby plans all the excursions and lets me know when it's time to get you. That's how it works. You know that perfectly well." And again Door started to close its eyes and even to fade a little.

"Don't get all huffy and fade out on me!" And before Door could fade any further, Corah reached over and turned the handle. Door had no choice and opened right up. Corah went through -- but then she remembered her manners and turned back to the door and said, "Thank you, Door."

Corah marched out onto the dock and looked around. Sure enough, Mr. Trilby was out there floating above her head just as he was the first time she met him. This time Corah had to call to him and wake him up.

Mr. Trilby shook his head, saying "Urga urg! What, what?!"

"Would you please, sir, punch your belly and float on down here so we could talk?"

"Ah, it's you, Corah. Do we have an excursion tonight? I don't remember one."

"No we don't. I'm sorry to bother you, but I would like a special excursion. Could you come down so we might talk?"

"Oh yes, of course. Give me a moment." He punched his belly. There was a hissing sound and he deflated and landed gently on the dock. "Now," he said, "What is it you want to talk about, my dear?"

Corah stood up straight. She announced that she had a story she wanted to write but the ideas wouldn't come to mind. It was going to be about pogo sticks ... maybe a bunch of pogo sticks... and there would be some funny creatures, but that was all she knew. So, she wanted to know if there was some place she could go and find ideas. "You see, I need some ideas about what those creatures might look like and how they would behave. Is there such a place?"

Mr. Trilby frowned and twirled his walrus mustache. He thought and thought. Finally, he raised his bushy eyebrows and held up his forefinger. He had an idea. He could go get his large Tour Book that had just about every place he could use for excursions. "I have a book," he announced. "Maybe that'll help. It's a complete Tour Book is what it is." He beamed with satisfaction.

"Oh, good! Where is it?"

Mr. Trilby frowned again and twirled his mustache. Then he held up his forefinger. "I know just where it is!" And he waddled off toward the far end of the dock. There he opened a locker and hauled out an enormous, fat book. He carried it back to Corah. He pulled out a tall table and put the Tour Book on it. Then he opened it up, which was not so easy, heavy as that book was. "What we might do is look in the index. First we need the right words to take us to the place we want." He tried a lot of words: idea, imagination, story, drawing, plot, images, creatures, and so on. They led to some inter-

esting places but none of them were quite what Corah was looking for. Finally, he tried the words "pogo stick." That worked! It took him to a place called the "Misty Mind Mine." It worked because the Tour Book knew what was on Corah's mind. It was just the thing. The Tour Book described the Mind Mine as a place deep inside a misty grotto and you could go in there and find ideas that were hidden in your very own mind. They were in your mind all the time but you didn't know it. And you could find them in the Mind Mine.

"Ah, listen to what it says here. You go deep into the grotto and in its blue light you will find things there, characters you invent, events you make happen and pictures you draw. That's just the ticket!" Mr. Trilby was very pleased with himself.

"Oh, yes, that's it!" cried Corah. "But how do I get there?" She was ready to go.

"Ah, that's not so very hard. We need to contact the Bard Lady. She'll take you right to it."

"Who is that? Do you know her?"

"No. Never met her. But she's in the Book and it says that only the Bard Lady can take people into the Mind Mine. What's more only people who have ideas are allowed. It's clear you do have ideas. So that's not a problem. Since she is in the Book, that means you can rely on her."

"How do we get her to take me there?" Corah was worried this might not work. She might not be available tonight.

"I'll call her on my little black excursion machine." He pulled a black box out of his coat pocket and punched a few buttons. Then he stopped and after a few moments the box spewed out a long piece of paper. Written on it was the Bard Lady's answer. "It says here that she'll arrive in seven and a half minutes rowing her punt."

"And she'll take me to that place you called the Misty Mind Mine?"

"Right!"

"Oh I'm so happy!" Corah wanted to hug Mr. Trilby but she didn't. Instead she thought for a moment, and then asked, "What's a punt? And why is the lady called the Bard Lady?"

"Bard means she deals with words, with poems and also stories. That is her specialty. Her punt is a low boat she steers and propels with a long stick. And here she comes." Mr. Trilby waddled back to the locker with his great Tour Book. Corah looked out into the dark waters and saw the little boat coming toward her. Standing at the back of the long, low punt was a lady with frizzy hair all over her head, a frumpy dress and a loose hanging sweater. She wore big floppy shoes with piled red and white stockings. She was using a long stick to bring the punt up to the dock. She got out and gave

Corah a big smile holding her arms out in greeting. "What a delightful young lady!" she said, "Who is this fine young person?" Mr. Trilby waddled back as quickly as he could and welcomed the Bard Lady. He told her how pleased he was to meet her and he introduced Corah.

The Bard Lady fairly beamed at Corah, saying, "So, shall we go together to that Misty Mind Mine? Now listen a moment while I explain. The Misty Mind Mine is in a sort of grotto you can only enter with a boat. It's a little dark in there but there is a bluish light that comes up from below. It's really beautiful and there you can meet your ideas, your inventions, your characters, your stories, whatever there may be in your mind that you hadn't known was there. Okay?"

"Okay! That's just what I want. Can we go there now? Can we?" Corah blurted out in her excitement.

"Certainly, get on board, dearie." The Bard Lady got on the punt at the back and took up her big rowing stick. Very carefully, Corah stepped off the dock and onto the punt. She waved at Mr. Trilby as the punt moved out into the dark water.

As they sailed along, the Bard Lady liked to sing little songs she invented on the spot. One went something like this:

Heigh high ho,

Here we go,

Punting along with a song.

We're free as the bees

That buzz in the trees,

On our way this special day.

We go on going

and ever rowing

We'll soon find what's on our mind

Heigh high ho,

Here we go,

Punting along with a song.

There were other songs, many of them, before Corah and the Bard Lady reached the grotto that contained the Mind Mine.

Entering the grotto was a little spooky. The ceiling was very low and they both had to duck their heads. The punt kept on moving through the mist and very soon a bluish light glowed from deep under the water. In the bluish light, Corah began to make out images,

ones that she had thought about drawing or putting into stories. One thing she always liked to do was to draw the top of a creature on a folded piece of paper and have someone else draw the bottom on the other side. When the piece of paper was opened many funny creatures appeared. They were always spectacularly awkward. Corah loved them and then she saw some of them bouncing around on pogo sticks. They seemed to be having a marvelous time. They grinned and shouted and laughed as they chased each other about. They were all different and crazy looking, their top halves and bottom halves looking really silly. They were all trying for longer and longer bounces. They gave Corah laughing fits.

Corah had an idea. She would write a story called "The Great Pogo Stick Race" and it would have a racetrack and judges sitting in high chairs and calling for the races to start and announcing the winners. The Bard Lady asked Corah if she wanted to stop a while and write that story. Corah asked, "Could I do that?" The Bard Lady pulled the punt up to a little platform. On it was a big black machine and a chair. The Bard Lady had Corah sit in front of the machine and put some wires to her head. When the machine started up, Corah saw all sorts of stories and she recognized them but never so clearly. She thought really hard for a while then quickly she saw the words form in her mind. That way, she wrote "The Great Pogo Stick Race" from beginning to end. She was so happy.

She turned to the Bard Lady and told her, "Now I have to get home right away before I forget the story." She was worried that she might wake up the next morning and the story would have faded away. So she asked the Bard Lady if she could get back to Mr. Trilby's dock right away. The Bard Lady agreed and helped Corah back in the punt.

Soon they were under way passing out of the grotto and its blue light. The Bard Lady made the punt go as fast as she could, but they were surrounded by mist that was building up thick enough to be a fog. Now Corah began to worry that they would get lost and never get home again. From off in the distance came a strange honking sound, something like a being horn. They also could see a light in the direction the sound was coming from. As they got nearer, Corah could make out Mr. Trilby holding a horn and a powerful flashlight. He was there to help them get home. Corah was very grateful to him.

Back at the dock, she thanked him for arranging another wonderful excursion. She turned back to the Bard Lady, who smiled that wonderful grin of hers and gave her a hug. Corah really liked that funny, dumpy Bard Lady and waved to her hoping the Bard Lady would find her way home, too.

Mr. Trilby told her he would go to the great Tour Book and arrange another fine excursion next time. Now however it was time to get back to her sleeping self in bed. She turned to Door. This time it smiled at her, saying, "So, you wanted a special excursion and you got one. I'm glad." Corah bowed her head a little and said she was sorry if she said anything annoying. Door said that she had been a little rude, but it understood how much she wanted to find that place for ideas, stories and pictures. It added, "I'm just happy it all worked out so well. Welcome back." Then it swung itself open to allow her through. "Good night," it said, "Sweet dreams."

Corah ran to her bed and jumped in. She started dreaming at once, and she watched her whole story as she slept. It was exactly as she wrote back in the Mind Mine. It made her smile in her sleep.

The next morning she woke happily just thinking about her fantastic excursion in the night and the wonderful story she invented. She went right to the computer and started writing at once. Even before it was time for breakfast, she had the story written. It was great. She spent the rest of the day drawing pictures of the funny creatures on their pogo sticks.

Excursion #6:

"Flying up to Mount Parnassus"

Some time in the middle of the night, while Corah was sound asleep, she began to be aware of a strange sound. The sound was slowly getting louder. It was a sort of flapping noise, but not the kind of flapping you hear from a helicopter. That would be a quick flapflapflapflapflapflap sound. This was more of a FLAP...FLAP...FLAP...FLAP sound such as a huge bird might make. The sound seemed to be coming very close, so close that Corah sat up and swung her feet out of bed. Then suddenly it stopped right outside her room. Then she saw Door appear gradually on her wall and then she heard Mr. Trilby's whistle.

Corah had been looking forward to a new excursion for several days, but just now she wasn't sure about going out the Door not knowing what animal was out there. It certainly seemed to be a very big bird. Door looked at her with big eyes as if he had seen something.

"Is there some big creature out there?" Corah wanted to know.

Door thought for a moment. "Yes but I'm not sure what it is. It's not a bird, I can tell you that. But it does have wings. And it is very big. And it's white. And there is someone sitting on top of it. I don't know how she got up there."

That made Corah a little apprehensive. She thought about going back to bed, but just then she heard Mr. Trilby's whistle. That meant that he did have an excursion ready for her. She reached up and turned Door's handle and peeked out.

Door said, "You might as well go on out. At least you can find out what that big thing is." Corah nodded her head and pushed Door open. Door closed itself right away. Out on the dock Corah looked up. Towering over her was a great white horse with wings and perched between them was a beautiful lady.

Then a strange thing happened. Corah looked up the other way thinking she might see Mr. Trilby floating in the air the way he liked to do. Instead there was a man fluttering his winged feet in the air and flying over to the horse. The man lifted the beautiful lady off the horse and brought her down to the dock. Corah turned and saw Mr. Trilby standing right beside her with a big smile.

"Do I have an excursion for you!" Mr. Trilby declared.

"Would you first do the introductions, please?" Corah was very correct about that.

"Oh, I do beg your pardon. This gentleman is Perseus. Next to him is his wife Andromeda. And behind her is his winged horse, Pegasus. And here is Corah. As I explained before, Perseus, I want you and your winged horse to take her up to the top of Mount Parnassus."

"What for?" Corah wanted to know.

"Excuse us for a moment, Perseus." Mr. Trilby took Corah aside. "Do you remember when you came back from the Mind Mine with the Bard Lady and I promised you that I would go to my great Tour Book and find another excursion? Well, this is it. I wanted you to see where ideas come from even before they might be found in the Mind Mine. So, Perseus will take you to meet the muses on Mount Parnassus. They are the ones that send inspiration to people – writers, poets, musicians, and so forth."

"Oh." Corah turned and looked at Pegasus. I'm going to have to get on that huge horse's back to fly up there? I didn't think horses could fly."

"This one can," said Perseus.

Corah turned to him. "I suppose he can talk, too."

"Don't be silly," said Mr. Trilby laughing. "Horses can't talk."

Corah was confused about this excursion. She didn't know what to ask. Lots of things went through her mind: What exactly are the muses? Why are they up on that mountain? What does Perseus have to do with all of this? And why is that beautiful lady here? And especially what does all this have to do with me? She didn't know what to ask first.

Mr. Trilby saw Corah's frowning face: "You want to know what all this has to do with you." Everyone started talking at once: "You see, there are people…" "They live up on the mountain…" "They're called muses… "There are nine of them…" "Except there is a tenth one that has been forgotten…" "They are all Perseus' half-sisters… "Yes, and their names are Clio, Melpomene, Thalia…"

"Stop, stop!" cried Corah. "If you all talk at once, I'll never understand anything."

"You're right," said Andromeda. "Sorry."

"I do apologize," said Perseus.

Mr. Trilby said he would take over because he knew what was on Corah's mind. "First of all, one of the muses has asked to meet you because of the art you make, your drawings and your paintings. She knows about you because she sends you ideas for your art and she likes what you do with them. She has always lived up on the mountain with her sisters who send ideas out to people down here below. Now Perseus here is their half brother and he visits them regularly. Finally, he saved Andromeda from a ferocious sea monster and now the two of them are married. So Pegasus belongs to Perseus and he and Andromeda belong to each other. Now that's what you wanted to know, right?"

"Except how do I get up on top of that big horse?"

"I'll get you there," said Perseus. He lifted Andromeda up and flew up above Pegasus. He settled her in between the great wings and went back down to Corah. "How about that?"

Corah laughed with delight. "All right!" And she thought to herself how great this was. She had already ridden on a griffin and on a unicorn. And now a winged horse! She held up her arms and Perseus lifted her up and placed in front of Andromeda on Pegasus' back. Corah marveled that Perseus could fly with just the wings on his feet, but he certainly could – and carry people like the beautiful lady up in the air.

Mr. Trilby waved as Pegasus began to beat his great wings and rose up in the air. "Have a good flight. I'll be here when you get back."

Perseus flew alongside Pegasus as they rose higher and higher. For a brief moment Corah could look down on her house on Parkview Avenue before Pegasus flew into a cloud and out the top, flying faster and faster, his great wings going FLAP...FLAP...FLAP...FLAP. Corah and Andromeda held onto each other, the wind whipping through their hair. After a while, Pegasus banked to the right passing over a towering mountain. Andromeda had to shout to tell Corah that that was Mount Olympus where the gods lived, included Zeus, the king of the gods and also Perseus' daddy.

Soon another mountain came into view. That was Mount Parnassus. Pegasus again banked and descended until he landed gently on the slopes of the great mountain. Perseus came alongside and lifted first Corah then Andromeda and placed them both on the ground.

Corah was a little out of breath from flying so far so fast. After a while she looked around, blinking in the bright sun. She saw that she was standing on a slope just below the summit of the mountain. And then she could make out several women standing or sitting on the slope above her. They were all holding things such as musical instruments, scrolls, or masks. Squinting she could count them. There were ten of them. Corah turned to Perseus and asked, "Do you know which one asked to meet me?"

"Well, I suppose it has to be the one who sends you ideas for your art. Let's see -- which one that would be?"

"Well, they're your half-sisters. Don't you know them all?" asked Andromeda.

"Yes and no. My mother was Danae and theirs was Mnemosyne. She named nine of them and assigned an area for each one: Euterpe for songs, Terpscihore for dance, Melpomene for tragic plays, Thalia for comic plays, Calliope for poetry, and so on."

"Those are really funny names," Corah declared.

"Oh, there are others," Andromeda said. "Polyhymnia, Clio, Erato, Urania..."

"That's just it. I have nine half-sisters with names and one half-sister without. The tenth one inspires artists, we know that, but no one seems to know her name. Over time people must have forgotten. Certainly you wouldn't think her mother, Mnemosyne, would have forgotten: she is the goddess of memory, after all."

Andromeda reminded Corah that it was this muse that wanted to meet her: "She is the one who sent you ideas for your art – like your cow bubbles."

"And my owl in the tree?"

"Right."

By then the tenth muse was running down the hill toward Corah.

"That's her, isn't she?"

"Yes," said Andromeda.

"And she doesn't have a name?"

"No. Maybe you'd like to give her one."

"I'd like that," said Corah as the tenth muse ran up to her.

"You must be Corah, the artist. I'm the muse of art – drawing, painting, sculpture. I am so glad to meet you. I really like what you do with the ideas I send you. You're very good!"

"Thank you." Corah wanted to be very polite and of course she was happy to hear what the muse had to say. But then she considered that introductions usually called for an exchange of names. "You know my name is Corah but I don't know yours. Perseus says you don't have one. Is that right?"

"Oh yes, he's right. I have been up on this mountain sending inspiration out to people with names like Phidias, Praxiteles, Leonardo, Rembrandt and Picasso. It's been centuries and in all that time I haven't had a name. It's really bothersome. Would you like to give me one?"

"You would let me do that?" asked Corah, very pleased. "It might take while, you know."

"Oh, no worry. I've been without a name for so long a few more minutes shouldn't matter."

"Well, I'll think about it hard. Meanwhile maybe I'll just call you Arty. How about that?"

"That's fun. It's certainly different!" She laughed. And so did Andromeda and Perseus. Pegasus didn't know how to laugh but he looked amused.

Then Arty took Corah's hand saying, "I want to show you something very special." She pointed to a building farther down the mountain slope. "That is a museum. A magical MUSEum."

"A museum? Why is it magical?"

The two of them began to walk hand in hand down to the building while Arty explained how it was magical. "Inside you can wish to see any great work of art and it will appear there all at once without ever having disappeared from its place down on earth. I'll show you."

When they entered the building, Corah was astonished. The first room was very large but also completely empty.

"Now we have to wish some particular works of art to appear

here. Then the room won't be empty. Let me think. Do you like the ballerinas that Edgar Degas painted?"

"I don't know," Corah had to admit.

"I'll show you." Arty snapped her fingers and suddenly the room was full of paintings of ballerinas, dozens and dozens of them.

Corah was amazed. She looked closely at several of the paintings and admired them in all their detail: brush strokes, compositions, and color. "These are just beautiful!"

They went into the next room and it too was empty. Arty called for the paintings of children done by Mary Cassatt and she snapped her fingers and again the room was full of beautiful paintings. Corah thought she could spend all day looking at the ways those artists created their works. In the very next room Arty snapped her fingers and paintings and drawings by Corah appeared. Right away Corah saw her painting of the owl in the tree and her drawing of the "cow bubbles." And over to one side she spotted "The Great Pogo Stick Race" that she had done after her visit to the Mind Mine. And there were many others there. Some were examples of her abstract art, some of her experiments with pointillism. It was fun to see them all together in a museum.

Arty announced that she had to get back to her place on Parnassus because she had a new inspiration to send to a particular artist.

As they left the room, the pictures faded away. The same thing happened as they left the other rooms.

When they were outside, Corah stopped suddenly and said, "I know now! I know your name. It's Artemusea. That's it!"

"That's wonderful. Thank you. 'Artemusea.' I like that. Now, be ready – I'll be sending you ideas for more art."

And so they hugged each other and as Artemusea went back up the slope, Corah ran to Perseus and Andromeda. "That's was awesome -- that museum! And that wonderful lady, the muse, I just love her. I can't wait to get home to my sketchbook. You know what? Artemusea (that's her name) she promised to send me ideas for my art. This is great!"

Perseus was impressed, saying, "Her name is Artemusea? You gave her that name? That's wonderful! After centuries at last the tenth muse has a name. This is big news for the whole world."

Andromeda smiled at Corah. Corah knew she had done something marvelous. Then gently Andromeda spoke, "I can tell you'd like to go home now. Are you ready?"

"Oh yes, please."

Corah lifted up her arms and Perseus picked her up and placed her on Pegasus' back. He did the same for Andromeda. Then Pegasus flapped his great wings and rose up in the air. Corah looked down and saw Artemusea waving to her. She waved back happily.

Pegasus banked to one side and flew with Perseus alongside. They passed over Mount Olympus and over the sea. After a while Pegasus descended through clouds until Corah could just make out her house on Parkview Avenue.

Moments later Pegasus gently landed on the dock where Mr. Trilby was waiting. With a big grin he welcomed Corah back: "Now how about that excursion?"

Perseus lifted Corah off Pegasus' back and brought her down to the dock. Corah beamed at Mr. Trilby: "It was the best. It was great. Wonderful!" She turned to Perseus and thanked him and she waved at Andromeda still high on top of Pegasus. She watched as Pegasus flapped his wings and rose up with Perseus beside him and then disappeared into the sky. She turned to Mr. Trilby and said she wished Sienna could make this same trip. She gave Mr. Trilby a hug and went to Door. Door smiled grandly and opened itself. Corah went in and joined her sleeping self in bed.

Of course the next morning Door was gone. Corah almost jumped out of bed. She ran to get her sketchbook. She found it and sat right down and started a drawing that she had thought up the minute she was awake. It was an idea that must have come from Artemusea. While she worked, Sienna came into her room rubbing her

eyes and asked her sister why she got up so early. So Corah told her all about Mount Parnassus and those ten muses. Sienna looked at Corah's drawing and said that Artemusea must be a wonderful muse.

Excursion #7:

"Castle on the Hilltop"

The night was still and dark and Corah was in her deepest sleep. In that deep sleep, she was dreaming happily about a beautiful castle. She didn't know what or where that castle was, but she knew exactly what it looked like because she saw herself drawing it. It was picturesque and surprisingly detailed. She smiled and the dream began to fade away, but she told herself that she would let Mr. Trilby know about it. Maybe in the morning she could draw the castle in her sketchbook just the way she had dreamt it. She began to get restless thinking about telling Mr. Trilby the dream. She turned on her side and then looked at the wall. She saw the door beginning to fade in, that door that was never there unless it was time for another excursion.

She studied her friend Door. By this time, Mr. Trilby ordinarily would blow his whistle announcing a new excursion, and Door would open its eyes wide to welcome Corah. But there was no whistle and Door had its eyes shut tight. She went to Door, put her hands on her hips and said in a loud whisper, "Hey, Door! Are you asleep?" Door didn't answer, so she went right up to it and knocked.

With a great rattling, Door shook itself awake. Its eyes opened wide and looked right at Corah. "Sorry. Must have dozed off. Didn't mean to."

"Well," said Corah, just a little impatiently, "What's going on?

Why are you here? And where is Mr. Trilby? Has he arranged an excursion tonight? If so, why hasn't he blown his whistle?" All those questions came tumbling out of her mouth. Actually, she had a lot more, but she clamped her hand over her mouth to keep them from coming out.

Door blinked a few times, as if it were trying to remember something. After a moment it blurted out, "Oh, yes! Yes! Well, it's like this. Maybe an hour ago, Mr. Trilby told me to be ready. He had some details to work out and then he would blow his whistle. I guess you got here before he was ready."

"With your eyes, the ones on the other side of you, can you see him?"

"Give me a moment…. Yes I do see him. He's out on the dock at a table and he's looking at a big piece of paper."

"Can you see what's on the paper?"

"Hmm…. It looks like it might be a plan for some kind of building."

Corah was excited. "Is it a castle, do you think? See, I was dreaming about a castle. Maybe that's it."

"Hmm…well…Yes, I think it might be. It might just be a castle."

"I want to go out there and see it. Do you think he could have copied the castle out of my dream? Let me go see." Corah took hold of Door's handle and tried to turn it.

"Now, now. I can't let you do that. You know you have to wait for his whistle before you can go out on the dock for the excursion of the day. I'm sorry but I am locked until the time comes."

Corah didn't know just what to do. She really wanted to know if that was her castle and if it would be part of the excursion. Finally she gritted her teeth and knocked loudly on Door.

"Don't do that!" protested Door. But just then there came a strange sound from the other side. It was a sort of CHUG-CHUG-CHUG-CHUG sound, like a choo-choo train.

"What is that?" Corah exclaimed.

Door paused while it looked out. Then: "It's a great tall machine with a smokestack and steam puffing out of it. There is a little man way up on top using a steering wheel. And it's towing a couple of trailers. It's really strange!"

Door unlocked itself as soon as it heard Mr. Trilby's whistle.

Corah pushed Door open and peered out. The huge engine with all its steam was chugging straight for the dock. It was so big and noisy that Corah had to step back. Mr. Trilby was there, helping the little man at the wheel pull up against the dock. When the great machine came to a stop, Mr. Trilby turned and saw Corah standing at Door. He came and took her hand and led her over to the machine. He told her that she was going to have a marvelous excursion.

He pointed to the windows in the first trailer and several little men waved at her. Then he pointed to the little man on top of the puffing engine. The little man waved cheerfully saying, "Hey, y'all! I'll be right there!" With that, he swung his legs over to the top of a ladder and started to climb down.

While Mr. Trilby watched him coming down, he told Corah about this new excursion he had arranged. "You are going to enjoy this one," he said. "See, I caught that dream you had about a castle and I put it on paper. It's over there on that table. This man is a master builder and he is going to make your castle his next project."

Corah was astonished, but, before she could say anything, the little man was standing in front of her. He was remarkably short — no taller than Corah herself. And he was squat, round and compact, wearing bib overalls and a yellow construction helmet. He ran his finger over his little moustache and beamed at Corah. "Heighdy, little miss!" (Corah thought it was pretty funny that he would call her "little miss.") Then he went on: "Mr. Trilby here, he told me you got yerself a plan – sompun like a castle, is 'at so?"

Corah looked at Mr. Trilby, who nodded. She turned to the little man: "Well yes. At least I think so." She couldn't understand how all this could have happened so quickly. It was only a moment ago that she dreamt of the castle. Now the plan is on the table and a master builder is ready to go to work on it.

Mr. Trilby stepped in, saying, "Corah, this gentleman is Mr. Billy Builder Bob and he is in charge of our excursion. He is going to work with you on building your castle. Now I need you two to come over to the table and examine the plan from Corah's dream. Corah turned to Billy Builder Bob and asked, "Is 'Builder' really your middle name?"

"Yep. It's because I love building so much I put that name in the middle between Billy and Bob. But you may call me just 'Billy Bob.'"

When they got to the table they started looking over the plan, Billy Bob making suggestions and Corah explaining what she understood. The plan on that piece of paper was exactly the way she saw it. Corah turned to Mr. Trilby and asked, "How did all this happen? How'd you get this castle plan out of my head? How did you get Billy Builder Bob to take on the project? How can any of this happen so fast?"

"Hey, talk about fast. We'll have your castle built today. How 'bout that for fast?" said Billy Builder Bob with a big smile. Mr. Trilby just nodded saying, "I have my ways." Then, after a pause, he added, "This man is a fantastic builder."

Corah made a little curtsy and said, "I am glad to meet you, Billy Bob." And he replied, "Well, I am just so pleased to make your acquaintance, Miss Corah." That said, they fell to studying the plan. Corah looked back and forth from Billy Bob to Mr. Trilby. Meanwhile, Billy Bob muttered, "Ummm...yeah, OK...yes, good!" and so forth until he finally declared, "That's a fine design. They don't build them like that nowadays. But I can do it and I know just where. You ready, little Miss Corah?"

"Oh, yes. Let's do get started."

"Oh, mustn't forget our workers. There are twelve of them and they can build a castle like this in no time at all. Just you wait and see." He went to the table, picked up the drawing, rolled it up and started up the ladder, urging Corah to come up on top of the machine. Corah hesitated looking up the tall ladder leading to the top of that great puffing machine. Mr. Trilby took her hand and

assured her, "This is going to be one of my finest excursions." He helped her start up the ladder.

"Come on up, little Miss Corah. I got a plot of land goin' be just right for your castle." With that, Billy Bob fired up his engine and it began to go CHUG-CHUG-CHUG-CHUG, belching great puffs of steam out the smokestack.

Seated up top next to Billy Bob, Corah waved at Mr. Trilby standing way down on the dock. The great machine moved off, pulling its bus trailer with the workers and, behind it, another trailer with all the building blocks and equipment, and behind that a big cement mixer. A strange thing began to happen as they entered into a dark valley. The sky began to grow lighter. It seemed the sun was about to come up. It was the dawn of a new day.

After a while, Billy Bob pointed to a high hill just ahead. "Up there," he said, "is where we goin' to build that castle of yours. Right up there on top of that hill." They came to the bottom of the hill and started the long climb to the top. It was so steep that they had to zigzag all the way to the top. When they arrived on top, the sun shown on them and they had a wonderful view out over the whole valley that was still rather dark.

Billy Builder Bob swung his legs over to the ladder. "Come along, Miss Corah. We got work to do." He scampered down and opened the door to the bus trailer. All twelve workers came tumbling out, each one short and squat with bib overalls and a yellow construction helmet. They made a circle around Billy Bob, who had laid out the paper plan on the ground. They chattered among themselves so fast that Corah, who was on the ground by then, couldn't understand a word they said. She assumed they were calculating how they would go about building the castle.

Suddenly, one of the workers shouted, "WHOOP!" and they all scattered. Three of them pulled piping out of the trailer and ran to

build scaffolding. Two attached a belt between the steam engine and a cement-mixing drum and started the drum rolling. Four of them starting hauling building blocks out of the trailer and three started putting the blocks in place. But they were working so very fast that all Corah could see was a blur. But she did see the castle growing. It seemed to get bigger and taller every minute. It was amazing. In fact, by the time the sun was setting in the west, a banner was flying from the top parapet. Corah admired it so much she had to sit down and just look at it. After a moment, she jumped up and ran into the castle and through all its rooms and up onto the ramparts. From there, she waved at the twelve workers who were resting after their hard work. She ran back down through the castle and out where she stopped to look at the building. She picked up the drawing from her dream and it looked exactly like the plan. She was so thrilled she dropped the paper and gave Billy Builder Bob a hug.

After detaching the belt from the cement mixer and the steam engine, the twelve workers tumbled back into the trailer-bus. Billy Bob climbed up the ladder to the driver's seat, followed by Corah. When he started up the machine, it made that same CHUG-CHUG-CHUG-CHUG sound as white steam poured out of the smokestack.

Billy Bob told Corah she made a good design and he added, "When we finish zigzagging down the hill and out into the valley, you can look back at your magnificent castle perched atop that hill. Yep, just you wait!"

Corah smiled. She was so grateful to Billy Bob and his twelve workers and she said so. After a while, she looked back at the castle. He was right. It looked magnificent. The valley was already dark, but the castle caught the last golden rays of the setting sun, making it look resplendent. Corah admired it with her own glowing smile,

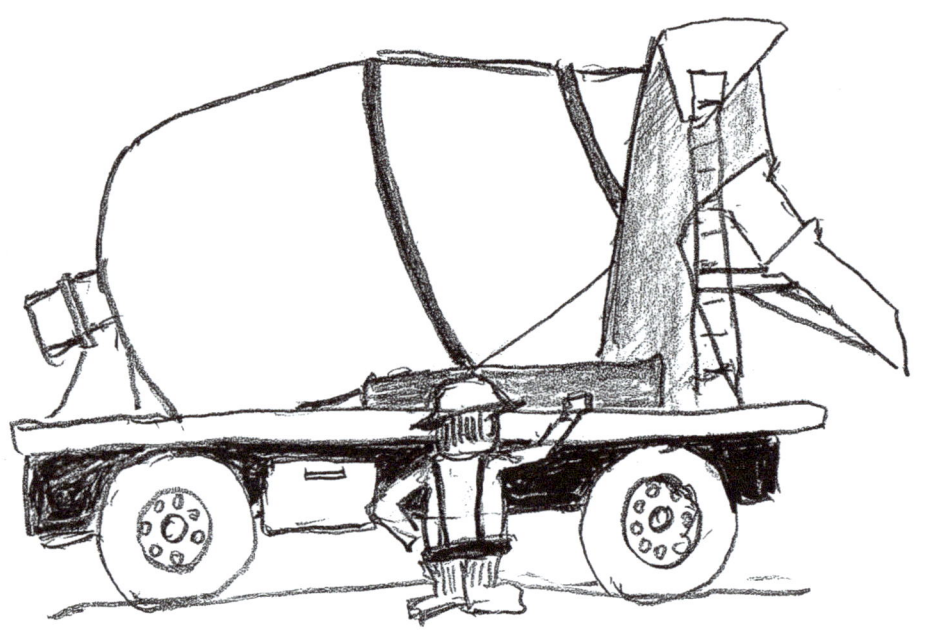

then settled back in her seat for the rest of the journey back to the dock.

When they arrived, Mr. Trilby was there to greet them and he called up to Corah, saying, "Now how about that for a fine excursion?"

"Wonderful! Just wonderful!" She scurried over to the ladder and came down as fast as she could. "Thank you, Mr. Trilby, thank you!" She looked at Billy Bob on top of the engine. "And thank you, too, Billy Builder Bob. You and those workers are great. I love that castle on the hill. Thank you!" Billy Bob waved at Corah and so did the workers through their windows in the trailer-bus.

Then the great engine puffed CHUG-CHUG-CHUG-

CHUG and turned away. After a while, it was out of view, but that CHUG-CHUG-CHUG-CHUG could still be heard. Corah thanked Mr. Trilby again and turned to Door, who opened itself for her and welcomed her home. She went through and Door closed behind her. Just before getting back in bed, she suddenly remembered she had left the drawing on the ground by the castle. She turned back. Door had already vanished. "*Well,*" she thought, "*I guess I can make a drawing of it in the morning.*" She joined her sleeping self in bed and went off into a happy slumber.

Excursion #8:

"Mythical Menagerie"

There comes a time in the night when everything becomes very still and quiet. At such a time the darkness is at its darkest. Then people slumber unaware of anything nearby. No doubt some of them are dreaming.

Corah was at that stage in her sleep as she became aware of a rattling sound. It gradually became louder and louder. Suddenly she sat up in bed. That loud rattling sound was coming from across her room. She squinted in the darkness. Over on the far wall she could just make out that Door was there. It must mean the time had come for an excursion.

Corah swung her feet down to the floor and rose from the bed, leaving her sleeping self behind. She could tell that the rattling was coming from Door itself. She made her way over to it. It was rattling against its own doorjamb. Door was shaking with fear, quivering in panic. Corah knocked, saying, "Door! What's the matter with you?"

"Oh, it's...horrible, ju...ju...just horrible!"

"What's so horrible?"

"Out there, on the d, d, d, dock."

"What's out there on the d, d, d, dock?"

"Oh, it's awful! There are two enormous sea serpents. They have raised their huge heads out of the water. They're towering over Mr. Trilby, who's right on the edge of the dock. I'm afraid they are going to gobble him up. Oh, I can't look. It's awful!" And Door closed its eyes tight.

"Don't be such a scaredy-cat! Turn around and look again. Tell me what you see."

"Oh, all right. I'll give it a try. I don't like it, but I'll do it." With that, Door flipped around, its eyes and mouth gone to the other side. At once it flipped back and looked right down at Corah without saying a word.

"Well? Is Mr. Trilby all right?"

"I can't believe it. Yes, he's just standing there looking up at those great serpents. Just stands there! Why doesn't he run away? Or he could do that trick of his and blow himself up like a balloon and float up and away from those monsters. But no, he just stands there."

"Let me have a look." Corah reached up to grasp Door's handle.

"Oh, no, you don't! You know the rules. You don't go out on the dock until Mr. Trilby blows his whistle. You know that."

Corah was getting a little exasperated, but just then she heard Mr. Trilby's whistle. Very reluctantly and very slowly Corah opened Door, but only just a crack. She peeked out. She couldn't believe what she saw. Just as Door had said, Mr. Trilby was standing at the edge of the dock looking up at the heads of two enormous serpents, their tongues flitting in and out.

"Ah, there you are, Corah. Come over here. We've got a fascinating excursion for you. You're going to like this one."

Corah blinked her eyes – partly because the sun was so bright on that side of Door and partly because she was so amazed. "You and those two monsters have an excursion for me? I don't want to be anywhere near those huge snakes. I'll stay right here near Door, thank you very much."

"You don't need to be afraid, dear Corah. First of all, they aren't snakes, if that's what's bothering you. Next, let me introduce you. Corah, this is Claude and Maude. They are a pair of sea creatures with long necks. Come and look."

So, ever so slowly, Corah walked over to Mr. Trilby and looked up. Then she looked down. She saw that those long necks were connected to big bodies with great flippers. They were both tied to a sort of sea chariot. And a man stood on the chariot holding the reins. The man tipped his Panama hat, saying, "Name's Mick. Glad to meet you."

Mr. Trilby announced that Mick had agreed to take Corah to his very special place. It's called "Mick and Mikayla's Mythical Menagerie." He added, "There is nothing like it in the whole world. You'll be amazed, astonished, and awestruck once you see the animals there."

"What's a menagerie?" asked Corah.

Mick answered from his sea chariot, "It is a collection of animals, a sort of zoo. Only the animals in this zoo are mythical." Corah studied the man. He had safari boots, a military jacket and a Panama hat. He had a nice face with a slightly crooked smile.

Corah blurted out, "Are you telling me that you have a collection of real mythical animals?"

"Yep."

"*Real* mythical animals?"

"Yep."

Corah looked at him askance. "That doesn't make sense. Mythical means not real."

"Yep. You're right. Mythical means not real."

Here Mr. Trilby interjected, "See, Mick and his wife Mikayla have a device that they use to create the mythical beasts. You have met some of them already. You remember Gregory the griffin who took you and your dog Odin past a castle with a flock of flying harpies, through the Woombah Wood and across the Sinkhole Plain and into the labyrinth, where you met the Minotaur and finally on to the hillside where you saw the unicorn? You remember all that?"

Corah had to admit that she did.

"And when you flew up to Mount Parnassus, who took you there?"

"Pegasus, the winged horse."

"Right! Well, Mick and Mikayla created all those animals."

"Really?"

"Yep," said Mick. "You'll get to see them when we go through the menagerie. At the end, we'll show you how we make these mythical creatures. In fact, we'll let you create one."

"Could I do that? Really?"

Mr. Trilby said, "This is one of the best excursions I have ever come up with. So, go ahead, climb down, get on the sea chariot and let Claude and Maude take you out to the island of the Mythical Menagerie."

Corah looked back and forth between Mr. Trilby and Mick as if to ask if this will be safe. Mick gave her his charming crooked smile and Mr. Trilby nodded. Satisfied, she climbed down and got on the sea chariot. Mick came after. Mr. Trilby said he'd be right here when she got back. Mick snapped his whip and the two sea monsters were off at astonishing speed, their huge flippers beating on the water.

Corah had to hold tight to the edge of the sea chariot as it bounced on the waves. With the wind blowing in their faces, it was a little hard to talk. Mick did manage to explain that he and Mikayla created Claude and Maude, but they're not really mythical beasts but extinct sea creatures. They're called plesiosaurs – more or less.

"A kind of dinosaur, right? They aren't mythical. They're extinct."

"Yep. You're right. But I don't plan on making any more dinosaurs. I'll stick with the mythical."

Then Mick told Corah to look ahead. They were getting close to the island. Corah could make out an archway with the words "Mikayla and Mick's Mythical Menagerie" written on it. In front of it was a dock and on that dock a woman waving to them. "*That must be Mikayla,*" Corah thought. The two plesiosaurs, Claude and Maude, brought the sea chariot up to the dock. Mikayla helped Corah up onto the dock. Corah saw she was a pleasant lady with a kindly crooked smile, only hers was crooked the other way from Mick's. Mick jumped up onto the dock, snapped his fingers, and Maude and Claude swam off.

Corah looked around when she heard a strange sound. It was a griffin looking straight at her. Corah recognized him at once. It was Gregory the griffin who had carried her on that long excursion looking for a unicorn. "Ha-row, Orah," he said. (His beak made it hard to speak clearly, but he was clearly happy to see her.) Corah reached way up and patted Gregory on the head.

The four of them, Mick, Mikayla, Corah and Gregory Griffin,

walked under the archway into a jungle with big ferns all along the path. "Ees wonafu, you wah see," Gregory announced in a sort of scratchy voice.

Eventually they came to a clearing. On the far side there was a very tall fence. Corah was convinced that there must be some big monster inside that fence. She went right up to it and pressed her face against the wire mesh, hoping to see what creature might be in there. She could make out a writhing form way far away and occasionally there was a belch of fire. Suddenly the form stood and rushed at Corah and the others. She had to jump back. It was a dragon and flames came

At that moment the dragon let out a tremendous roar and belched a fireball into the air. Corah was so surprised she sat right down and Mikayla had to help her up. The dragon sort of chuckled and beat its bat-like wings as it trotted off. No sooner was Corah on her feet than a large harpy landed on a branch just over her head and let out a terrifying screech. It was a large harpy but, like the smaller ones Corah had seen flying around the castle, it had a bird's body and a woman's face. Mick spoke very harshly to the harpy, warning it not to bother visitors ever again. The harpy harrumphed and flew off.

"Are all the creatures here so scary?" Corah wanted to know.

out of its mouth. Mick said not to worry because the dragon was on the other side of a moat and his flames could not reach the fence. Still, Corah could not help being afraid, for it towered over all four of them, making growling noises as it spat fire.

Over the noises, Mick remarked, "This is one monster that I have yet to tame. He's very obstinate but sooner or later I'll have him calmed down so only smoke will come out his mouth. Anyway, that is our dragon. We used to have others, different species, you know, but now they're all erased. I don't think I want any more dragons, yep -- no more."

"On, no, no," Mikayla assured her. "We have many smaller, gentler creatures. Come this way. We'll show you." And Mick and Mikayla walked onto another path with Corah and Gregory following. That path led them into a deep forest where tall umbrella trees towered over them and put the path into shade. They came to a sharp turn in the path. There they came on a patch of sun shining down on a curious creature. He was looking straight at them, his face that of an old bearded man. He spoke in a gruff, gravely voice, saying, "How do you do?"

Corah thought that was amusing and replied, "Very well, good

sir, and thank you for asking." Then she noticed that the man's head was attached to a lion's body with a long narrow tail that had a scorpion stinger at the end. Corah turned to Mick to ask if this creature was dangerous.

Mick answered, "No, not at all. This is a manticore. He's a miniaturized lion, you see, and he has been trained not to use the scorpion stinger. Feel free to chat with him if you like."

Corah turned her attention to the manticore and asked, "I hope we haven't blocked your way as you seem to be out for a stroll."

"Oh, not at all, dear lady. It is my pleasure to meet you. May I ask your name?"

"Of course. I am Corah. And you, sir?"

"They gave me the name Manny, I suppose because it goes well with manticore. Manny Manticore, don't you know? You seem to be a natural human being. These people, Mick and Mikayla, they haven't created you, I suppose."

"Don't be silly, Manny. Of course not," said Mick

"Well, you do create a lot of the animals who live here. Just wanted to be sure. Why are you here, young lady?"

Mikayla said, "She is doing a tour of the menagerie."

"Ah. You are here to see all manner of cockeyed beasts with parts of different animals thrown together, like this fellow here with his

eagle head and lion's body. Crazy."

Gregory snorted loudly. He was really proud of his appearance. Manny looked at him, said, "Pardon me," and then padded away on his lion paws into the forest.

"What a very strange man...or whatever you call him," Corah remarked. Just then the harpy flew just over her head screeching loudly. Corah ducked and said, "I really wish she wouldn't do that."

"I'll have to have a talk with her," Mick promised.

"Corah, dear," Mikayla announced. "Let me show you a funny little beast. I think it'll amuse you. It's called a muscaliet. Come this way."

They all set out on another path. After a while they passed into open countryside with a green pasture. Corah could just make out that beautiful unicorn grazing in the distance. She remembered it fondly because she once rode on its back. Further along they encountered a centaur who was eating apples off a tree branch just over his head.

Just then Gregory the griffin looked up in the sky and cried out, "Howtch out! Harsee come!" Sure enough, the harpy flew down onto the branch above the centaur who promptly galloped off in alarm. This time Mick was really annoyed. He called the harpy to come down to the ground. He spoke very sternly and the harpy flew down. She tucked in her chin and looked ashamed. Mick reprimanded the harpy. "I am sorry, Mister Mick. I promise to behave," she muttered meekly.

After that, Mikayla told Corah about the little creature called a muscaliet. She said, "You can even hold it in your hand. She led the way to a small cage, a sort of rabbit hutch. She reached in and brought out a little furry creature. It was like a rabbit, but it had very tall ears on its head and boar's tusks in its jaws. It had a bushy tail, much like a squirrel's. Corah picked it up to cuddle it, but suddenly it surprised everyone by letting out a strangely quiet roar. Corah thought that was funny and tried to imitate it.

Mikayla asked Corah if she would like to create her own creature. "Oh yes!" Corah was enthusiastic. "Where do we start?" Mikayla said they should first put the little muscaliet back in its hutch. Then she and Mick led the way to a large white box that had a door like a freezer door.

Mick told Corah that she would have to go inside the white box. "There," he said. "Mikayla will close the door. Then she will put a box over your whole head." Mick stopped and looked at Corah, who was frowning. "Is something the matter?"

Corah thought for a moment. "I don't think I would like to go into that white box, and I doubt I would like the door to close, and I know I wouldn't like to have box put over my head."

Mikayla patted Corah on the back, saying, "Well, we don't have to do this. Maybe you'd rather go on home. Gregory the griffin will fly you back to the dock and Mr. Trilby."

Gregory added, "Ah tay oo ohm," and he tossed his head for emphasis.

Corah thought for a few moments, then asked "Well, could you tell how it will all work?"

Mick answered, "When your head is in that box, you have to imagine a creature. Once you have it in mind, you hold up your finger, and Mikayla will adjust the size to be fairly small because you really don't want a monster. Then she will take the box off your head. When she puts it on the floor, your invented creature will come out."

"All right. And then what?"

"Well," said Mikayla, "then it can go with you down to the dock and see you off."

Mick added, "You see, we don't keep all the creatures we create. They very soon fade away just as if we erased them. If we want to

keep one, we just spray it with a magical fixative and it will join our menagerie."

"All right. I think this will be interesting. Let's try it."

So Corah and Mikayla went inside the white box and closed the door. Corah sat in a soft upholstered chair and Mikayla put the imagining box over her head. It was a big black box, much more comfortable than Corah expected. Mikayla told her to start thinking of an animal and then to add parts of different animals to it. She was to hold up one finger when she had finished imagining a mythical animal of her own. She started to imagine an animal. It began with a pig. She gave it a pig's snout. The image of that pig was right there in front of her as if on a movie screen. She went on imagining and gave the pig four tall chicken legs and a donkey's tail.

Corah started to laugh at the funny looking creature and, to make it funnier, she added a silly set of little wings on its back. With that, she laughed and held up her finger.

Mikayla took off the box and laid it on the floor. She explained that a real breathing version of her imagined animal would come out of the box. But she also warned her that the animal will fade soon and self-erase. Corah could have fun with it for a while before it disappeared.

Corah was disappointed. "Can't you do something to stop it from disappearing?"

"It can be done with a fixative solution, but we have strict rules about not adding new mythical creatures. Now, watch this."

Just then, the box pushed a creature out and it was just as Corah had imagined it. It had a pig's head, a couple of small wings, four tall chicken legs and a donkey's tail. Corah was delighted. It was just the right size and exactly as she had imagined it. She went and opened the door and the piggy creature came out with her.

"So you like it?" asked Mick.

"Oh, yes! Yes!" Corah and the piggy creature ran in circles around each other, the piggy creature snorting all the time, making Corah laugh.

Mick announced that it was time for Corah to go to the dock

and be on her way home. She patted her piggy creature on the head. Then Gregory the griffin knelt down for Corah to get on. Mick and Mikayla marched with them to the dock. There the harpy flew down to the ground in front of them and asked pardon for being such a nuisance. Corah told her that it was all just fine now and not to worry.

She looked down and saw the piggy creature fading slowly away. She was a little sad and said goodbye to it. Then, when she waved to Mick and Mikayla, Gregory took off into the sky.

He flew over the water for some time. Eventually, Corah saw what looked like a round balloon on the horizon. When they got closer, the balloon turned out to be Mr. Trilby who had blown himself up, as he sometimes did, and was floating high up in the air where he could spot Corah coming home. Corah saw him punch his finger in his belly. She heard a hissing sound as he shrank to normal and settled on the dock. Gregory flew down and landed gently beside him. When Gregory knelt down, Corah got off. "Now," asked Mr. Trilby, "was that a fascinating excursion or was that a fascinating excursion?"

"That was a fascinating excursion!" And Corah laughed. She turned to Gregory and thanked him for the ride. He bowed his head and took off, flying back over the water. Corah smiled and thanked Mr. Trilby. She went to Door who said it was glad she was home and opened itself. Waving back to Mr. Trilby, she went in and joined her sleeping self in bed, very happy with her latest outing and her piggy creature invention.

Excursion #9:

"Interplanetary Travel"

ORAH WAS DREAMING. SHE FLOATED GENTLY AMONG wisps of white clouds passing her by. It was very pleasant. She smiled. But then a shrill sound intruded on her dream. It certainly did not belong there. It was terribly shrill and really irritating. But then she realized it was Mr. Trilby's whistle, the one he blows when he has an excursion ready for Corah. She sat up in bed and looked. Sure enough, Door was there, and it wouldn't be there unless it was time for an excursion. Naturally, she jumped out of bed.

Leaving her sleeping self behind, she ran to Door. Door looked at her with stern, squinty eyes: "About time you got here. Mr. Trilby has been whistling out there and all you would do is shift around in bed. So, are you ready to open me and go out on the dock?"

"Oh, yes! But tell me what this is all about. Do you know?"

"No," replied Door. "That is for you to find out. Has Mr. Trilby ever let you down? You couldn't have a better tour director. You know that!"

"I do know that. But just for me could you turn your eyes around to the other side and tell me what you see out on the dock?"

"Very well, but you could just open me and go out on the dock and see for yourself." Door's eyes and mouth disappeared for just a while and then reappeared. Door looked at Corah. "Mr. Trilby is

out there at his table, looking at big charts or maps or diagrams. I can't tell which. He is talking to a strange squat man with whiskers that stick out all over. And he's wearing a long black gown and a four-corner hat. Funny looking man!"

"Anything else?"

"Well, yes. There is something else. Right next to the table there's a tall clear plastic tube. It must be wide enough you could get inside.

That is, if you wanted to. Funny looking thing!"

Just then the whistle sounded. Corah jumped. She grabbed hold of Door's handle saying, "I better get out there on the dock." Door opened and she ran out onto the dock. Just as Door had described, there was a big plastic tube and a whiskered man. The man was sitting on a stool at the table showing Mr. Trilby one of the charts.

Mr. Trilby looked up. "Well, sleepy head, there you are at last. You have to meet an old friend of mine. He has made a stupendous discovery. In fact I'd say it's truly earth shattering. And he's willing to share it with us in a new excursion!" Then Mr. Trilby turned to the whiskered man. "This is my friend, Earnest Astor, or I should say Professor Astor. He's a genius. Thanks to him, this is going to be the most astonishing excursion I have ever arranged. You won't believe how fabulous this will be, Corah. Professor Astor, this is Corah." Mr. Trilby added, "Corah likes excursions, and, Corah, you are going to like this one."

Professor Astor did something that startled Corah. He jumped off his stool and ran right up to her, saying, "I am so glad to meet you, Miss Corah. Will you come with me on an interplanetary journey?" By now, he was shaking Corah's hand.

"This is going to be amazing!" declared Mr. Trilby. "You are going where no man has gone before!"

"Oh," said Corah.

"'Oh'? Is that all you can say? Just 'Oh'?"

"I mean, what is interplanetary travel? Is that what you do?"

Professor Astor smiled. "Yes, that is what I do. I travel from one planet to another. Some are a lot more interesting than others."

"And listen," Mr. Trilby interjected. "The one we will visit is really interesting."

Now Corah was intrigued. "You really know how to get to other planets? Aren't they all terribly far away?"

"Miss Corah, you are absolutely right! Some of the planets scientists have discovered are so far away you couldn't get there in your lifetime."

"But," said Corah thoughtfully, "we only have a night time."

That made Professor Astor laugh. "Oh, Miss Corah, you're absolutely right again. But, see, I have a solution for that problem." Then he started to pull out some of those charts that were lying on the table.

"Wait, wait!" Mr. Trilby interrupted. "Let's keep to basics. Corah, this man, this genius, the Professor, has made a discovery that no one, absolutely no one, knows about. There is a planet on the other side of the sun. We can't see it because it is always hidden back there. No one knew about that. No one!"

That made Professor Astor laugh again. "Yes, no one. Now you might say it will take a long, long time to fly around the sun and catch up with that planet. And you'd be absolutely right again."

"Professor Astor has invented a wondrous device. And you are going to visit that planet right away!" Mr. Trilby enthused. "Best excursion yet! Wait till you hear this."

Professor pointed to the plastic cylinder. "This is my invention. It is a teleportation device."

Corah was a little dubious about all this. First of all, she thought it very strange no one but this professor has ever known about that planet. Then she wanted to know what "teleportation" meant. So she asked, "What's teleportation?"

Mr. Trilby answered at once. "It is like television, which sends moving pictures from far away. Or telephone, which sends sound from far away. 'Tele' means far. So teleportation means sending people far away."

"You're going to send me far away?" Now Corah was getting uneasy.

"It's not as though you haven't been far away before," Mr. Trilby insisted. "Think about it. Remember Cloud Eight? Or down under the sea? Or Mount Parnassus? Or the labyrinth of the Minotaur? They were all far away. And you came back from all of them. You'll

come back from this one too. Oh, it'll be fantastic! I can't wait!"

By this time Professor Astor had opened the cylinder's door and he was holding a black box that had all sorts of buttons and dials on it. "You see, Miss Corah, you simply step inside the tube here and close the door. I'll step in with you and push the buttons for our voyage. Next thing you know, we'll both be on the planet."

"Isn't that great?" Mr. Trilby could scarcely contain his enthusiasm.

"Well, I'll tell you one thing." Corah was very serious. "You had better not lose that black box while we're out there. It makes me nervous."

"Here, I tell you what, I'll come with you. All three of us will travel to the planet. And I will make sure the black box is safe. It won't get lost. How about that?" Mr. Trilby was ready to go.

Corah was amazed. She had never seen Mr. Trilby this excited and certainly never heard his wanting to join an excursion. While she pondered this behavior, she suddenly noticed that Mr. Trilby was gone. He had disappeared. He had been standing right next to her. She looked to the right and to the left, up and down the dock, but he was nowhere.

"Here!" Corah and Professor Astor looked up. Mr. Trilby was floating above them, all puffed up just as he was the first time Corah met him, the time when she sailed out to the island for tea with Mrs. Molmy and Mrs. Balmy. Surely he wasn't planning on blowing a sailboat out to the planet.

"Sir," called the Professor. "Sir, be so good as to come back down here while I explain a few things."

"Oh, very well." Mr. Trilby punched his finger in his belly and there was a hissing sound as he slowly descended to the dock. Meanwhile, Corah (who had to stifle a laugh) decided to ask a few questions of her own. For example, what is the planet's name? Has Professor Astor been there? What is it like? Do people live there? Are there any animals? And she very quickly asked all those questions before Mr. Trilby settled down onto the dock.

"Those are good questions," remarked Professor Astor. "To answer you, first of all the planet has no name. You could give it one if you like, once you've seen the place. I was there and I can tell you it is like a pleasant garden with plants and flowers and trees, but not like anything you have seen. But there are no people there, just some strange and likeable animals. You'll meet some of them, too." Corah liked that idea. Then the Professor added, "I have one more very important matter to tell you. The air on the planet is very thick. You can breathe the air, but you can also swim in it. You'll see some animals doing that."

By now, Corah was almost as eager as Mr. Trilby to be teleported to this new planet. She blurted out, "Let's go! Can't we leave now?" Mr. Trilby agreed. "Let's be on our way."

So Professor Astor took up the black box and opened the clear plastic cylinder. It was a tight squeeze with all three inside, especially because of Mr. Trilby's big webbed feet. Corah and Professor Astor

had to stand on those feet, but it did not seem to bother Mr. Trilby.

Then the Professor pressed a few buttons on the black box. There was a loud "WHOOSH" sound and a play of lights, and suddenly they were on the planet looking out at the landscape and the sky. An animal, with a set of flippers and fins and feet, swam up to the plastic tube, looked in and smiled at the three inside. Then a strange thing happened: the animal settled down on two feet as if to wait to meet the people. Very tentatively, Professor Astor opened the door and the three came out. They faced the animal who was just their size. For a short while they looked at the animal and it looked at them. Then the animal nodded its head, smiled broadly and made a sort of bow. The Professor also smiled and bowed. The animal seemed satisfied and walked off.

Once it was gone, they all took a deep breath of that thick air. They were there! They actually were on the planet on the opposite side of the sun. They all shook their heads and cast their eyes about in wonderment. What an awesome world this seemed to be! The sky above them was luminescent with waves of light of many colors crisscrossing each other. It was beautiful. Then looking down they saw all kinds of trees and bushes and blossoms. Corah had never seen plants like those.

Corah was spellbound. Suddenly she took a notion. She jumped up and started swimming in the air. She swam up well above the other two. She was always a good swimmer and she did flips and dives and twists, laughing all the while. Gradually, she became aware

that there was a smiling creature swimming right along side her and smiling as it too did flips and dives and twists. And soon the two of them were laughing with delight.

Mr. Trilby called up to Corah, saying, "Would you please come back down to us?" So Corah patted the little creature on the head and floated back down. The three of them, Corah, Mr. Trilby and Professor Astor, set off down a path leading through a grove of unusual trees and alongside of a variety of plantings on the hillside. As they walked, a flock of creatures flew over them -- or a school of creatures swam above them. In either case they were all smiling. They encountered others on the ground. In one meadow there were ten or twelve creatures standing on their hind legs to watch the

group go by. They too were smiling. This was a very friendly planet.

They came to a place where the path made a sharp turn to the right. They could hear loud noises coming from around the corner -- noises that sounded like something smashing hard. They soon saw what was causing the noise. They found themselves at the top of a cliff. Looking down, they saw huge waves crashing against the rocks. The noise was like thunder. Professor Astor was not so surprised for he had been in this place once before. He explained that the sound was so intense because water was thick, just as the air is thick. In fact, the water is so thick you really cannot swim in it. It is much safer to swim in the air. And if you want to have a drink of water, you have to chew it.

While they were admiring this thunderous water they became aware that there was a smiling four-legged creature nudging them with its nose. It would nudge one of them and then run back toward the corner, look back at them, then do the same thing again: nudge, run and look back, nudge, run and look back. Clearly, it wanted to take them somewhere. So they did follow the charming little creature, who led them back toward where they had started.

As they came close to the clear plastic tube they saw a group of smiling animals, surrounding a table laden with fruits and nuts and vegetables. They also had glasses full of flavored air to drink. The

animals chattered cheerfully and they nodded and smiled. This was a welcoming table. So, of course, Professor Astor, Mr. Trilby and Corah happily joined the group. Corah was very surprised that the food, especially the fruit, was so delicious. Mr. Trilby worried that the food might not be good for human beings, but Professor Astor reassured him that he had tried it before and it had no ill effects.

The Professor stood up and addressed the crowd, saying, "I would like to convey to all of you our deep and heartfelt gratitude for the gracious hospitality you have shown us. Each of us says 'thank you, thank you, and thank you.'" With each 'thank you' they bowed their

heads in a gesture of appreciation. And the animals all bowed their heads in acknowledgement even though they hadn't understood a single word the Professor said.

With that, the Professor opened the door to the plastic tube. For just a moment Mr. Trilby seemed alarmed and he started patting himself all over. Finally he said "Aha! There it is!" He pulled the little black box out of one ,of his pockets. Mr. Trilby handed it to the Professor.

Now the three crammed themselves into the tube. The door closed. The animals waved and smiled happily. The three did their best at getting their hands up to wave back. The Professor pushed the buttons on the black box. They heard the same WHOOSH sound and saw the same multicolored lights they had seen when they left the dock. In a matter of minutes they were back on that dock. Everything was just as it was when they left. It was as if they never went anywhere whereas they must have traveled millions of miles.

They stepped out of the plastic tube. Mr. Trilby was so thrilled, he again floated up into the air. Meanwhile Professor Earnest Astor turned to Corah. "Did you think of a name for the planet?"

"Oh, yes. I think I know the name of the planet."

When Mr. Trilby heard her say that, he punched himself in the belly and came down to the dock with a brief hissing sound. "Wasn't that great! What name did you give it?"

"I thought of a lot of names, like 'Wonderworld' or 'Pleasnet' but I didn't like any of them. That place reminded me so much of Adam and Eve in the Garden of Eden. It was so peaceful and beautiful that it made all the animals smile. I thought of the Garden of Eden. So I took the two words, 'animal' and "Eden' pushed them together and came up with 'Animeden.'"

"Animeden! That's great. Just right. Animeden! Miss Corah, that's it! It's perfect," Professor Earnest Astor declared. "Just perfect!"

Mr. Trilby grinned broadly. "Corah, you've done it. That's exactly the right name for that planet. How I wish we could go back and tell the animals about the new name."

"Except they wouldn't understand you," Corah observed. "They don't speak our language. Besides, they don't know anything about the Garden of Eden."

"I hope we can keep it that way," said the Professor.

Mr. Trilby suddenly burst out with a declaration: "The name of Astor is going to be famous! Wait until the people here on earth hear of your discovery! It will cause a sensation. Everyone will be talking about Animeden. Everyone!"

"Yes, everyone." The Professor was suddenly very serious. "Think about that. There will be a mad rush as they try to get to the planet and once they do, awful things will start happening. That sort of thing has happened before. And you know it."

Corah nodded. She surely did know. She thought of humans taking over and harvesting crops, mining minerals, corralling the animals. They will behave like invaders claiming the whole planet as their own.

"I can see that Corah understands. Listen, do you think the three of us can keep it a secret? Keep the news from getting out?"

Now Mr. Trilby looked somber. Very slowly, he answered, "Yes, we can keep it a secret, but for how long? Sooner or later someone else will discover the planet. We won't be able to stop it. Dear friend, Earnest Astor, you deserve the credit and the fame of this discovery, but if you wish to conceal it from the world, someone else will show up claiming the discovery. It is inevitable."

"You're absolutely right." The Professor walked to the table and rolled up the maps and charts. He turned to Mr. Trilby and said, "I will teleport myself home. Maybe we can make a few visits while the planet is still a paradise." The Professor entered the clear plastic tube, punched some buttons on the black box, and WHOOSH, he was gone.

Door suddenly called out: "Hey, was it a great excursion?

Corah looked at Mr. Trilby and Mr. Trilby looked at Corah. Then they both said, "Yes, it was great." Corah went to Door and opened it. As she passed through, Door looked at her, saying, "Doesn't look like it."

Corah turned back. "No, it was wonderful, but we know something that beautiful can't last."

Mr. Trilby called out, "Good night, Corah."

Corah called back, "Good night, Mr. Trilby." Then she climbed back in bed to join her sleeping self. As she settled down, she recalled swimming in the air on the planet Animeden, and she smiled with a sense of satisfaction.

Excursion #10:

"Floating to the Elysian Fields"

CORAH HAD AN UNEASY FEELING. IT STARTED WHEN she went to bed. She glanced at the wall where Door would usually appear and she wondered if her unease had something to do with her next excursion. But then she reminded herself that Mr. Trilby's excursions always made her smile. It had been quite a long time since her last excursion, the one to Animeden on the other side of the sun. Perhaps it was time for a new one. Thinking those thoughts, she drifted off to sleep.

Sometime in the night she became aware of a rattling sound. She listened and finally decided that Door might be making that sound. She remembered the Door rattled like that when it was so frightened about the serpents that seemed to threaten Mr. Trilby. It could be that Door is alarmed by something else out on the dock. She sat up in bed and saw that Door was there and really did seem to be rattling. Corah felt she ought to do something. She swung her legs out, put her feet on the floor and walked to Door. Door was looking down toward the floor. It looked preoccupied.

"Is something wrong?" Corah asked.

"What?! What?!" Door was startled.

"Something wrong?" Corah repeated.

"Oh! No, nothing wrong. You have a new excursion. That's all."

"So? Well, why don't you open and let me go out on the dock?"

"Well, maybe I should say there IS something...shall we say? Something...unusual about this excursion."

"Well?" Corah prompted Door to go on.

Door turned his eyes away and then came back to look at Corah. "Well, for one thing there are three people out there on the dock and one of them you haven't met."

"Who are the ones I have met?'

"One of them is Mr. Trilby, of course. The other is Loblolly Joe. You remember him with the blimp? He took you up to Cloud Eight in his blimp. I guess he's here to take you on this new excursion."

"Yes I remember. He talked all the time. He was always talking. Who's the one I haven't met?"

"I can't say. He just showed up. Never saw him before. I heard him say he's here to give comfort."

"Who's uncomfortable? Nevermind. Just open up and let me go out there."

With a sigh, Door slowly opened and Corah went out on the dock. As soon as she did, Loblolly Joe waddled over to her and started talking. As Corah recalled he was such a talker, you'd have to interrupt him vehemently to get him to stop. So off he went: "Ah, Corah, there you are. I've been waiting for you. You see, I have the blimp here to take you on your new magical excursion. Mr. Trilby

asked me to come lend a hand, so to speak, not that a blimp is anything like a hand. You remember me and our trip up to Cloud Eight, do you? It was a great trip with people playing tennis on that cloud, and you...."

"Loblolly Joe, do be quiet for just a moment," Mr. Trilby interjected. "I need to talk with Corah about this new magical excursion." Then, turning his attention to Corah, he started to tell her about this night's destination. But before he could say very much, the other man on the dock interrupted and moved in front of him.

The man wore black trousers, a black frock coat, black shoes and a black hat.

"Pardon me," the man said, "but I do need to counsel with the young lady. This is a day that may trouble her." Then he turned to Corah, put his hands on her shoulders and looked intently into her eyes. This astonished Corah, who stepped back. Still he kept holding her shoulders.

"Now, Miss Corah, I want you to know that I am here to render aid and comfort. You know that, don't you?"

Corah blinked. "No, I don't actually."

"Let me explain. My name is Mortimer, Mortimer Modlen, and I am here to give you assurance that you do not have to be sad. I do understand. But let me tell you that you can be glad...now hear me... you can be glad because he is going to a better place."

Corah pulled away from the man and looked at his face. What struck her was his crooked smile that seemed to be frozen. It never changed. Then she asked, "What are you talking about? Who's going to a better place?"

Mr. Trilby gently took Mr. Modlen aside, saying, "Please, you are just confusing her. Give me a chance to speak with her about tonight's magical excursion. You're jumping the gun." Saying that, he ushered Corah to the far end of the dock where they could talk quietly. "As you know I have sent you off on many excursions. I went with you only once when we went to Animeden, the planet on the other side of the sun. Well, this time, I am going on my own excursion and I want you to join me there."

"Oh." Corah thought for a moment and then asked, "Is this a trip to a better place?"

"Well, it is a very beautiful place. It is called the Elysian Fields. You recall how from time to time I'd puff myself up into a floating ball? Remember? I did that when you went off to have tea with Mrs.

Molmy and Mrs. Balmy. You can see I am already a little puffed up."

"Oh yes, I remember. It was a long time ago. You puffed yourself up and blew my boat over to the island. But why do it now?" Corah was getting very curious.

"I'll do it so I can pass over to the Elysian Fields. I'll wait there for Loblolly Joe to bring you in his blimp. He knows the way."

"But." Corah did not know quite how to say this. Finally she determined to ask, "But why does that man, that...Mortimer Modem or Modern...why does he think I need his help?"

"Is it my turn now?" Mortimer Modlen stepped forward. "I mean this is the sort of thing I do. I explain things to people when one of their loved ones passes over."

"Please, sir, give me a few more minutes with Miss Corah." Mr. Trilby turned to Corah. "You see, the Elysian Fields are just stunning with blossoming trees, beds of flowers, bubbling streams, waterfalls tumbling into sky blue lakes, and soft, gentle breezes. You'll love it. That's why I want you to come on this excursion. I'll have the chance to watch you enjoy it. Tell you what: why don't you run get your little dog, Odin? We could have him come and run through the fields. We'll have such a good time."

Up to this moment, Corah had been worried because everything seemed somehow ominous. But this idea of running through such beautiful fields wiped all that concern away. She jumped up and ran to Door, who opened for her. Then she ran out of her room and downstairs, calling Odin's name. He didn't come right away, but she found him sleeping on a little table next to the sofa in the living room, a place he particularly liked. She quickly picked up the little dog. She bounded back to her room and to Door. Out of breath, she could barely ask Door to open. She then went out on the dock. There, right in front of her, stood Mortimer Modlen with his crooked smile. Looking behind him, Corah saw Mr. Trilby was now a round ball floating away. Now she again felt things were worrisome.

"Loblolly Joe," she called. "I want to go after Mr. Trilby. Let's go." And she handed little Odin to him and started to follow him to the blimp.

"Permit me," said Mortimer Modlen, blocking her way. "I have a role to play in Mr. Trilby's passing, and that requires me to ease the pain of loss that I am sure you feel."

Corah heard Loblolly Joe gasp, "AAAH!" She looked at him, then at Mortimer and back at Joe. After a few moments, she summoned up the courage to ask the question: "What is going on here? You say things like 'going to a better place' or 'Mr. Trilby's passing' or "the pain of loss.' When people talk like that, it's because there's something they can't quite say."

"Well, as for me," Loblolly Joe gulped. "All I can say is what Mr. Trilby told me. He said this will be his last excursion. That's all he said."

"AHEM," Mr. Modlen cleared his throat. "I, uh, I wouldn't say he's *dying* in so many words. Let's just say he's going away."

"He's dying!" Corah said this quietly but emphatically. After a brief moment she said, "I want to go to him.... Now!" With that, she ran to the blimp. She started up the rope ladder to the blimp's cabin and Joe followed holding little Odin. She looked back at Mortimer Modlen standing at the bottom of the ladder. He was saying something about being available to give aid and comfort. "Thank you, sir," Corah called down to him and added, "All I want now is to get to Mr. Trilby out on those fields he talked about." She pulled up the rope ladder and Loblolly Joe started the sputtering engine. The blimp set off for the Elysian Fields.

The ride was beautiful, and Corah looked down on green pastures and dense forests as the blimp rose up into the sky. She saw all that but felt anxious about Mr. Trilby. They might get there too late. After what seemed a long while the blimp sputtered to a stop right against the edge of the Elysian Fields. The moment Loblolly Joe opened the door, Odin bounded down onto the fields and ran off. Corah was worried he'd get lost, but he kept coming back and then running off again. She admired the lush landscape, sensed the fresh and scented breeze, and heard the chirps of many birds. She saw spread out before her an array of trees in blossom, gardens of flowers and in the distance two lakes, one with a waterfall tumbling from a cliff. The beauty of it all had her transfixed.

As she scanned this wonderful world, her eyes suddenly landed on Mr. Trilby. He was here, after all. She was so relieved that she had to wipe a tear away. He was there, seated on top of a large boulder. He was looking right at Corah and smiling broadly. He gave her a

little wave. Corah ran as fast as she could to that boulder. Mr. Trilby held out his hand and helped her up to sit with him. They sat together for a long while. Then, her eyes brimming with tears, she asked her dear friend, "Why didn't you tell me?"

With a deep sigh, he answered, "I know I should have, dear, dear Corah, but I just couldn't. When Mortimer Modlen, that dour fellow, stopped you to tell you not to be sad, you looked so bewildered, I wanted to pretend we were just going about our business. I know that was foolish."

Corah stared at him. She had never seen him in this light. For a moment it seemed to her that she was looking at the boy he once was. She wanted to say something to him, but she couldn't think what. Odin came bounding back, and sat at the base of the boulder. Mr. Trilby smiled at him and then took a ball out of his pocket. He threw it up in the air. Odin ran after it while it made crazy bounces that kept the dog running in all directions, trying to catch it. "It's a magic ball," Mr. Trilby announced, laughing at the antics of that energetic little dog.

Corah looked back at Loblolly Joe standing beside his blimp, ready to take her home. That made her think that she might not have much more time. She turned to Mr. Trilby. She got up the courage to ask the question she had wanted ask: "Mr. Trilby, would you tell me what is it like to die?"

"No. I can only tell you about myself. I felt a stirring deep inside my head, something that seemed determined to get out. I felt it swirling in there. Sometimes it made me forget how to talk. The words would fly off and I couldn't catch them. It's still in there, swirling about. But then, of course, finding myself in the Elysian Fields tells me that it will happen soon. This place is a way station to paradise. Knowing that is a comfort."

"But I am here, too. What about me?"

"Oh, you're fine. Once I move on, Loblolly Joe will take you back to the dock. I am so glad you are with me. I have done a remarkable thing arranging this last excursion for you. Some day you'll return here to be welcomed. For now it is a place for us to bid each other farewell. Life is full of many joys." Mr. Trilby looked out over the fields and saw Odin come running back, the magic ball in his mouth. He sat down at the base of the boulder, and Mr. Trilby laughed and clapped his hands.

"So this really **IS** our last excursion?"

"Ah, you will have many of your very own. You'll take trips, engage with adventures, and have many experiences in your lifetime. Some of them will bring disappointment, some will bring joy -- some might bring both. But now I must pass away." He hugged Corah. He began blowing himself up. He rose into the air over the Fields. Loblolly Joe came and stood next to Corah still seated on the boulder. Together they watched him float gently away over the trees and into the distance until he became only a dot in the sky. And then even that was gone.   Corah jumped down from the boulder and picked up Odin. Weeping, she turned and ran to the blimp. Loblolly Joe said, "That was such an extraordinary and caring man, that Mr. Trilby. Imagine that! He created so many excursions for you and now

created one for his very own self." Odin wiggled, as he often did, and jumped into Corah's arms.

Loblolly Joe then helped her into the blimp and started it up. Sputtering, it turned and flew back over the pastures and forests to the dock. There, he helped her down. He brought Odin down and the little dog came to Corah. Strangely enough, Loblolly Joe had nothing more to say. Instead, he returned to his blimp and sputtered off.

Corah went to Door, who stuttered, "Wonderful man! I expect that you will always remember the excursions he arranged for you, especially this last one." Then he paused. "Well, you probably can guess why I was rattling earlier. I knew what was about to happen. I knew."

Just then Corah and Odin heard a knock on Door. They were all surprised. Who could that be? Door opened itself. Standing there was Sienna. For just a moment they all stood there staring at one another. Then Sienna ran to Corah and hugged her, saying, "Is what happened what I think happened? Is Mr. Trilby gone?" Corah nodded. The two sisters held each other.

Door looked on with sad eyes, then he blurted out, "There may come a day when I'll appear again in your bedroom wall. And then we'll see what will come of it."

"Oh, I do hope so," said Corah

Door added, "I am to tell you that Mortimer Modlen sends his deepest condolences. You may call on him at any time."

"How do I do that?"

"I really don't know." Then Door opened, and Corah, Sienna and Odin went in. Sienna left to join her sleeping self in her room and Corah climbed into bed. Odin jumped up and cuddled beside her. Just as she was about to fall asleep she looked at the wall. Door had gone.

Author Note

These tales were written over the span of ten years as birthday presents for Corah Longman, beginning when she was five. One can perhaps sense her growing up over those years by the progression of the stories. During that time she herself took to writing stories and creating art. She is the daughter of Ian and Anna Longman and the older sister of Sienna, who has her own series of stories.

The following pages are some drawings for you to color…